NEVER ALONE

NEVER ALONE

MARGARET M SMITH

CHRISTIAN FOCUS PUBLICATIONS

© 1993 Margaret M Smith
ISBN 1 857 920 201

Published by
Christian Focus Publications Ltd
Geanies House, Fearn, Ross-shire,
IV20 1TW, Scotland, Great Britain.

Cover illustration by Maureen Eadie
Cover design by Donna Macleod

Printed and bound in Great Britain by
Cox & Wyman Ltd, Reading, Berks

CONTENTS

CHAPTER 1

'For this...tears are not enough,' Eilidh thought as she looked down on her mother's still face.

"She's no longer with us," the nurse whispered, the calm-professional voice gone.

How absolutely, how completely, she was no longer with them! The 'she' was empty of her, totally. 'But if she is not here, then,' Eilidh wondered, 'where had she gone? Where is she? Where is she right now?'

Eilidh looked across the bed at her twin brother, Paul. His eyes roamed around the side ward and he moved his hand slightly, as if to try and feel his head. His high-cheekboned profile was disturbed from time to time by flickering frowns, brief contractions of the forehead. But he was a tough fifteen-year old Londoner and he wouldn't cry in front of any starch-and-sympathy nurse. Eilidh knew that Paul would do all his crying alone.

"C'mon, I'll make us all a nice cup of tea," Nurse Williams said and quietly led them out of the room and into a small sitting room. "Sister has contacted your mother's cousins, and they should be on their way by now. Milk? Sugar?"

'What do I feel?' Eilidh thought, sipping the tasteless hospital tea. She shifted her weight on the hard plastic chair and puzzled. 'Do I feel anything? Is this the real grieving or - or had that happened before mum died?' Maybe they did their grieving while she was swiftly withdrawn from their little world. Into the hands of doctors and dope and delirium. 'So, maybe we don't have any more grieving to do,' she wondered, deep behind a frozen face.

So, death had happened. In spite of Eilidh's weeping and often blasphemous prayers, in spite of her denial and then her rebellion, in spite of her bargaining, her mother had died.

Almost as if reading her thoughts, Nurse Williams leaned forward in her chair and said in her soft, pillowy voice. "It's sad for you, I know that. But not for her. I mean, your mum's now in heaven, isn't she?"

Paul shot the nurse a look meant to crack concrete and told her that her imagination was working overtime. And if that flowery stuff was all she could say then she could take a hike.

As she listened to the twistings of her brother's mind, Eilidh felt she didn't know this voice. And maybe she no longer knew this Paul either. But she managed to hiss, "Don't use that kind of talk, Paul!"

"Why not?" he shouted. "What garbage!" The air around practically sizzled with anger as he continued flinging verbal grenades in the direction of Nurse Williams. "Who do you think you are anyway - Billy Graham? A nun in disguise? Whoever you think you are, get this - we're just sick of all those do-gooders who don't know their way out of a paper bag. Save your do-goods and words of cheer for someone else!"

Eilidh wondered if the nurse was counting to ten in the ensuing silence. Or maybe one hundred. Or maybe she was planning to strangle him with her stethoscope.

Nurse Williams merely let out her breath as if she'd been holding it all the time, and said, "I'm sorry. I suppose I wasn't seeing it from your point of view."

"You can bet your stiff starched cap that you weren't." His voice was like a fist. "If you were, you'd know that we're now orphans. Yeah, orphans!"

"Orphans? But isn't your father - "

"Oh, yeah, the old man is still alive. Somewhere. But he could be in Timbuctoo for all we know - or care."

"Yeah, he didn't care for us, did he?" Eilidh challenged, her gaze level and unflinching. "Took off with that skinny blonde just before Ellis was born."

"But there must be other relatives, surely?" Nurse Williams asked.

"Not really," Paul faced her fiercely. "Aunt Helen - mum's only sister - died years ago. And, right this minute, mum's two first cousins will be slugging it out. Not over who's going to have the pleasure of looking after us. But who's going to have the pleasure of NOT looking after us!"

Eilidh opened her mouth to protest but Paul checked her with an upraised hand. "It'll probably be Lucille and I hate her glossily packaged guts. The way she looks down her nose at us as if we were something she'd spotted at the bottom of her dustbin. She likes Ellis because she's just three and dead cute, but she despises us as a pair of lowly little nerds from the wrong side of the city. Once we reach sixteen - whoosh, that'll be us. On yer bike, fend for yourselves!"

His voice became strangled and he sagged like a punctured balloon into the nearby armchair. The fierce face softened and became almost childlike.

"Would you rather I left you alone, Paul?" Nurse Williams asked, trading a female-to-female look with Eilidh. Paul jerked his head up to stare at her. He shook his head no. And after a moment had ticked by, he was able to answer "No."

Eilidh stood up slowly, shaking her head from side to side, and crossed over to the large fifth floor window. Outside, the neon lights gloated harshly across the vast city. Away in the distance the glow from an industrial estate splashed the sky with murky orange, and down below knots of pedestrians rushed obediently forward at the green traffic signal. Everybody rushing. Paying no attention to anybody. Just wanting to go where they were going.

"Paul's right," Eilidh said, not turning round. "We're left alone, and I don't believe in your God, or any God. I used to believe before...before all this. Now, I don't believe any longer! If there is a God, then he is evil. Look what he did to mum. And now us." The bitterness rolled around her like a fog, and she fed her own anger, like heaping coal onto a fire to keep off the chill. It was easier than starting her season of tears.

"I can understand...why you both feel so bitter," Nurse Williams said. "But God could change that bitterness for you, if you just let him - "

"Oh yeah - wanna bet?" Eilidh said, still staring down at the screaming, shining lights. She turned round to face them, and the enormous pane of glass shone dark behind her head, the darkness of a city night. "Just stop...trying to understand and all that. Okay?"

"Okay." Nurse Williams rubbed her forehead in a contemplative way. "There's something your mother said to me last night. It's running about on the surface of my brain. Blow! What was it?"

Before she could go any further, the door opened and Cousin Lucille and her husband Jeremy were ushered in by a nurse. The faultless appearance of the couple gave out messages of wealth and opulence; from her rich, honey-blonde hair to his neatly-trimmed moustache, from their well-cut clothes to their impeccable hands.

The man now offered Eilidh a hand like a dead animal and sprinkled a cold smile over her. He had a horrible habit of coming up close so that contact with him usually had a smothering effect. Eilidh backed away as he murmured, "My dear, we are so sorry, so very sorry. Your poor, poor mum."

His wife, oozing gentility out of every pore, said nothing, but attempted a benevolent smile. It took her a few minutes to give up waiting for the twins contribution to the conversation, finally saying, "We're glad you're both being so sensible. We don't want to upset little Ellis, do we now?" Cousin Lucille had all the sympathy of a cement mixer.

Paul had never been a brilliant conversationalist and wasn't about to start now, so Eilidh agreed meekly, "No." Out of the corner of her eye she saw Nurse Williams at the door, silently beckoning her to come out to the corridor. Eilidh excused herself and followed her.

"I remember now!" Nurse Williams whispered.

"Remember what? ...Oh, you mean what mum said."

"Yes. It was just before she lapsed into a coma. It was so sudden! I mean, one minute she was well enough to make plans for going home to you and then...."

Eilidh felt her body wanting to fold up with tiredness. She didn't even have the energy to appear interested, but she managed to trot out, "Well, what did she say?"

"Something like...who will love my children when I'm gone? Then there was a lot I didn't understand - she had just had her shot of Diamorph, you see, and was a bit sleepy - but I did make out that there was a letter for some man. And it was in a drawer. Oh dear, it doesn't make much sense, does it?"

"No," Eilidh said. "It doesn't make much sense."

CHAPTER 2

"It doesn't make much sense," Eilidh muttered as she looked at her mother's writing on the envelope. Who WAS this John Paterson? And where on earth was the Isle-of-the-Unpronounceable Name? What did it all mean?

There was nothing else for it. She'd have to steam open the envelope and now was as good a time as any. Ellis was asleep, Paul had taken off after the funeral which had been earlier that day, and Cousin Lucille and her creepy husband were in the living room.

She crept into the poky kitchen of their tiny flat and switched on the electric jug. 'I could be Sherlock Holmes himself,' she thought grimly, 'if Sherlock Holmes was a nervous wreck.' She stood above the jug, aiming the steam at the envelope, and tried hard not to think of her mother's presence in the kitchen. All that sharp, quick energy as she moved about, apron clad, stirring, adding, tasting; busy, but always having time to give the help and attention that shaped her older daughter into the person she had become. Right now, though, Eilidh wouldn't allow herself to think thoughts of her. Her imagination might try, but she'd cut it right off, send on a substitute. Ellis, Paul, ANYBODY.

The letter began, 'Dear Mr Paterson. You won't know me, but I'm Helen Sanderson's daughter - '

"Daughter...Aunt Helen's DAUGHTER!" Eilidh let out a stunned whisper and, taking a backwards step, stumbled over the laundry basket. She regained her balance, and fighting for composure, carried on reading. She read her mother's explanation of her terminal illness, and her anxiety about her family's future. 'If at all possible could you look after the children till the older ones have finished their schooling? I know nothing about you, or your circumstances, and I only ask out of sheer desperation, believe me! If you are willing even to consider it, please contact me or the vicar I left legal papers with.' The vicar's address was enclosed.

Her heart, unaccountably, had begun to knock at her ribs. The letter was dated 10th April. A week ago - the day before their mother was rushed to hospital!

Cousin Lucille's voice called out her name, and for a moment, Eilidh felt dislocated in time. "Eilidh, have you any idea where that brother of yours is? Eilidh?"

Eilidh stuffed the letter into the pocket of her jeans and turned round to face Lucille's squirrel-like face with it's bright, inquisitive eyes. From up close she studied Eilidh as if she had only one chance to learn everything about her. "Um sorry, no - I've no idea," Eilidh answered, hoping to soften the anticipated acid comment.

Lucille wrinkled her nose with a show of distaste. "It's not good enough, you know - worrying us tonight, of all nights. Jeremy and I feel so drained after the funeral, and we wanted an early night. And especially since we had arranged a dinner party for Jeremy's clients tomorrow night." In the face of Eilidh's silence, Lucille lifted her eyes upwards as if appealing for the gift of patience. "You will manage here by yourselves for just the one night, won't you?"

Eilidh could have given several answers, but all of them were rude. Just then, however, she heard the noise of the lift stopping on their floor.

"That'll be Paul," she said, allowing the relief to leak out. Racing out of the door, she made her way into the narrow, dusty landing flavoured with Coke trickles and cigarette-ends. She only came to a halt when she bumped into a rather large policeman who was ushering Paul out of the lift.

"Paul!" she cried.

"Paul!" Lucille's voice rose a scandalised octave as she followed closely behind Eilidh.

"Is this your son, madam?" the policeman asked her.

"No! I mean, no, he's my cousin's son, that is, my late cousin. Joan, his mother, was buried today...poor Joan...." Her voice trailed away. It was a good performance, mourning dished out as easily as cream from a jug.

The policeman hemphed and humphed and looked uncomfortable. "Oh! In that case - "

"What HAS Paul done?" Eilidh demanded, cutting him off.

"Smashed a few windows in that empty factory down the road. We could overlook it this time, I suppose. In view of the circumstances."

The pause which followed could be described as pregnant. But once Lucille had left them to escort the policeman to the lift, Eilidh turned on her brother. "Have you got rocks in your head, or what? What made you go and do a crazy thing like that? Why?" She kept at him, adding fuel to her fire. She needed to understand.

"Sorry."

"Terrific! Since when did saying sorry make someone suddenly innocent?"

"Oh, keep your halo straight," Paul said, and gave a dismissive movement of his hand. "Don't go all maternal on me. You're only my sister - not my mother. Remember that!"

Paul looked at his sister, challengingly. He looked at her face, all the parts of it. The heavily-lashed, dark eyes, accentuating the finely chiselled features of her face, the swirl of dark hair emphasising her nervous, incessant movement, the angry spot of colour burning in each cheek.

"I'm sorry, Eilidh," he said, and there was an echo of shame in the words, "I didn't mean to take it out on you. I -"

Lucille re-appeared. "Aren't you going a little heavy on the drama, Paul?" she asked, looking at him with the offhand interest she might have shown a naughty puppy. She then looked towards Eilidh, or rather, through her. Right through without a flicker. Inquisitiveness replaced with indifference. Lucille wasn't easily cast in the role of the caring cousin; in fact, Eilidh felt like a school-child who had been shoved in front of the headmistress.

"We'll discuss this in the morning," Lucille said, before opening the door to the flat.

"At least, Cousin Lucille hasn't made a favourite of one of us," Eilidh whispered to Paul as they trooped back into the flat. "Equal-opportunity disdain. I can handle that."

Once settled down in bed, however, Eilidh found she couldn't handle anything. She lay in the dark feeling her life had been cut through with an axe. The cold, frightened feeling lay all around her body, like a wet blanket. She wrapped her arms around herself and longed for the morning. Beside her in bed, little Ellis was asleep, closed safe and tight in a cocoon of sheet and quilt; her dilapidated panda lying abandoned beside the shadowy darkness of her tousled head.

'What are your troubles going to be when you're fifteen, little girl?' Eilidh silently asked the little face. What'll be the very worst problem? A pimple that won't go away, a choice of boyfriends - or no choice at all! - or simply where to go on a Friday night?

Finding the silence in the flat suddenly oppressive, Eilidh quietly slid out of the bed and made for the kitchen for some hot milk. The door of the living room stood wide open, admitting a quadrilateral of light onto the hall carpet. Jeremy's loud, decided tones floated out.

"Close the door before they hear you!"

The door was flicked to a close. In the sudden flood of darkness, Eilidh stood stock still beside the ugly, unfunctional hall stand, and caught on to Lucille's sharp words "...just a delinquent!"

"My, you have got a clear grasp of the obvious, my dear."

"Oh, do be quiet!"

"I will if you will. Look, I quite agree with you. The boy is definitely a case of arrested emotional development and he'll corrupt our own boys within one day and what will our neighbours think? You've said that yourself a hundred times...but what are you going to DO about it, Lucille dear?"

"Nothing. I mean, we'll have nothing to do with him! Chantelle in Devon absolutely refuses to have him either - she says she's got her girls to think of, and that's worse."

"Talking of girls, what about Eilidh? She's quite an attractive young thing."

"Oh, yes, Jeremy! It's obvious to me you've noticed that much." Lucille said with a fine, needle-like contempt in her voice that pierced even through to Eilidh's ears. Lucille, Eilidh noticed, could instill towering venom into the name Jeremy when the occasion required.

"I'm not staying around listening to this!" Jeremy fired back. The door suddenly opened and Jeremy's stocky frame filled the doorway. Eilidh, with a chill sensation at the pit of her stomach, ducked down beside the hallstand. Jeremy whirled round once more on his wife and spoke, this time in an agitated whisper, "Think ahead, my dear. If you want to hold on to little Ellis - and you've always said a little girl would complete our family - then you'll need the older girl to help you. Am I right?"

Passing inches away from Eilidh, he crossed the hall to the bathroom. Eilidh dropped her head, and soundlessly, backward step after backward step, she made her way to Paul's miniscule bedroom.

Her face quivered and almost collapsed as she shook her brother awake. She wanted to talk and it couldn't wait till morning.

"Paul, please wake up. WAKE UP!"

"Mum...? What the...HEY!" Paul managed a strangled noise as Eilidh clamped her hand firmly across his mouth.

"Shut up, and listen! We've got to get away from here, and tomorrow night is our only chance. LISTEN!" She heard a trace of hysteria creep into her voice. "I want you to go looking in the atlas - for an island."

CHAPTER 3

Paul and Eilidh checked the atlas once again as they sat on the Glasgow-bound night train.

"It's over 700 miles away, but it's quite straightforward really. Another train after this one, a bus to the coast, and then a boat. Here's hoping the village isn't too far from the ferry terminal..." Eilidh's voice, almost a monotone, betrayed no excitement. Somewhere in the past hours, the weariness from a sleepless night had retreated; numbness anaesthetized anxiety and pain. She could think quite clearly, almost abstractly. She was standing on some tower overlooking the drama, a viewer as well as a participant.

Beside her, Ellis was enjoying her 'fix' - a thumb in her mouth, a hand running through Eilidh's hair. She removed her thumb. "Are us going to op-sital to see Mum?"

Eilidh momentarily bowed her head to avoid looking at those solemn, liquid-brown eyes. "Uh no, lovey. We're going to sleep in the train tonight! Won't that be fun?"

Eilidh couldn't look at her sister without her heart feeling soft and her smile spreading over her face. She liked the way Ellis's eyes rested on her face, trusting. She

liked the way the soft brown curls escaped from the teddy-
motifed bobble.   Concentrating on feeling maternal, she
became painfully aware that this was a motherless child.
"Poor little scrap," she whispered to Paul.

"What's a poor little scrap?" the little girl asked, and
the carriage, which they had to themselves, filled with
unexpected laughter.   Ellis was too sleepy to join in,
saying with a yawn, "I'm tired in my eyes...I didn't go to
bed for a long day."

"Close your eyes, then" Paul ordered.

The brown eyes opened wider.   "Do we 'ave to close
our eyes before we sleep?"

"Search me," Paul grinned.   "Say your prayer or
something."

After she lisped her prayer,   "Now I lay me down to
sleep I pray the Lord my soul to keep...", Ellis slept. Soon
they were speeding through the light-spangled darkness
towards a place they'd never seen and a dream Eilidh
believed in with desperation. Crazy with excitement - and
sad and lonely and scared.

'If only I could pray like Ellis,' Eilidh thought wistfully
as she looked out the train window. Catching a glimpse
of her profile reflected in the glass, she knew her mood
swings were like that of a tornado gone amok. Now she
felt defiant. 'What's the use?' she argued silently. 'I
prayed non-stop for Mum. No, from now on, when it
comes to prayer, I'm a conscientous objector.' Beyond
her reflection, beyond the window, it looked like it was the
scenery that was on the move, not the train. The shadowy
shape of trees shot past them at speed until they melted
into an undistinguishable blur. And then miles of passing

darkness, a darkness lit by the occasional all-night garage, the occasional distant village or small town, the occasional security lights of a large factory.

Paul laid down the atlas and leant back on the prickly plush of the head rest. "It's a long, long way, Eilidh. To the land of men wearing kilts and of people who toss the caber and say wheneffer and whateffer and how're you th' noo?"

Eilidh, laughing, said "Oh Paul, do me a favour! What you know about the Scottish islands could be written on the back of a bus ticket!"

"Ha, ha. Seriously though, what if this guy doesn't want us - what then?"

"For starters, I don't think mum would have written to him without good reason. Plus, if it's a total disaster, we'll just have to come back here. I told Cousin Lucille in that note that we were invited out of the blue to a friend up north...that we'd be back in approximately a week... that the address was enclosed - "

"Which you forgot accidentally-on-purpose, of course."

"Of course. Anyway, we've enough money for the return journey plus a week's worth of food. Between what was in the housekeeping jar and what people gave us at the funeral, it should do."

"If there was a league-table for sly guys, you'd be right at the top, sis. And to steam open the envelope...shocking and scandalous!"

"Hey, don't be so selective with your righteous indignation," Eilidh teased. "Who smashed those windows, huh?"

"It was a lesson in Elementary Survival," Paul fired back, throwing her a devilish grin. "You see, it was either an inanimate object - window - or dear Jeremy's face."

Eilidh's smile evaporated. She didn't want to say anything. Even having Paul mention him made the carriage dark, as if the outside darkness had seeped up into the carriage. But how could she ever share with Paul the effect Jeremy had on her? The mixture of loathing for the man, the inexplicable self-disgust she felt when he looked at her in that way - no, Paul would never understand. After all, wasn't he of the same sex?

"What I can't work out," she said, changing the subject, "is why we were brought up to believe that Auntie Helen was mum's sister - instead of her...her mother."

Paul wiped the sweating windows of the carriage before he lowered the blinds and shut out the night. "Perhaps Mum herself didn't know anything about it. Who knows? - she may have found something when she was going through Granny's bits and pieces last year."

"You mean - after Granny died in the nursing home?" Eilidh asked and her brother nodded.

A whole sea of unexplained happenings and mysterious occurrences seemed to have rolled between them and their mother's past. Later, as the train sped on northwards through the night, Eilidh was held on a threshold between dream and reality, with thoughts of the shadowy and featureless John Paterson. Who was he? What was he like? Was he young, old, married, single, nice, not-so-nice ...? Mulling over the meaning of it all, she fell into forgetting sleep.

They woke up to find that the darkness had slowly leaked away, and they were only minutes away from Glasgow's Central Station. Glasgow's unfamiliar buildings were suffused with gold as the little family emerged into the cool, sweet, April morning. A sleepy Ellis stuck out her lower lip like a wash-hand basin and flatly refused to walk. A taxi then had to be hired to cross the short distance to Queen Street Station, and by the time the northern-bound train slid out of Glasgow, dawn had given way to full-strength morning.

Ellis instantly cheered up when she realised that breakfast was to consist of Coke and crisps. She spent the rest of the journey pointing "what's that?" at everything that slid by. They'd have all of ten seconds to work out what she meant before she spied something else. In between, Eilidh managed to appreciate the scatter of patchwork fields, bathed in soft tingling sunshine, and then the miles mesmerized her as the spacial area of land and sky went through minute-by-minute alterations. Magnificent wooded scenery and turquoise lochs gave way to Highland glens, where the delicate sludge colours of heather and bracken were often broken by an apologetically winding ribbon of grey road.

A quick stop in a tired Highland town and then they were off again, this time on a bus journey to the coast.

The late afternoon sun was settling comfortably on Eilidh's shoulders as she alighted from the bus at the ferry terminal. Paul, adopting a breezy manner, set about finding the ticket office. With Ellis straddled over one hip, Eilidh walked over to the harbour edge where the sea was shallow, creeping softly, with emerald waves breaking into shimmering lacework against the boats.

"Bath? That's not a bath, is it Eilidh?" Ellis's voice was hushed, like the waves.

Eilidh laughed. "Oh, Ellis! Of course, you've never seen anything but Docklands, and that was ages ago. No, it's the sea...isn't it fantastic? And look, look over there, that's the boat we're going on."

Eilidh tried to imagine what was awaiting them over on the other side of that boat journey. It wasn't easy. She sighed and turned to watch as the people made their way slowly down the boat's gang-way. Many of them were met by friends and relatives and there were hugs and kisses and words of welcome. All at once she felt herself shrivelling inside, and was appalled at the pang of lone-liness she felt. She yearned for someone to care for them, yearned for the past, and for the way things once were. Her mind and her body called out for the security of the past 'come back, don't go....' Resolutely, she stamped on these thoughts, and swinging Ellis up onto her shoulders, she made her way over to the boat.

"Hey, miss, hold on a moment!" An authoritative voice from behind made her break her stride and turn round. A policeman, several yards behind her, shouted again, "Yes - you, miss! Wait a minute - "

Eilidh didn't want to wait one second. There was no power in her body or her mind that could have made her wait. She plunged into the milling crowd congregating around the gang-way. As one unreasoning thought raced after another through her mind, she pushed past people almost violently, giving way to the simple primitive desire to put as much distance as she could between herself and the Uniform.

Up the steep gangway, balancing haversack, bags and Ellis, she finally tottered weakly over to a deserted bench on the top deck. Isolation from the herd was what she now wanted above all else. But where on earth was Paul? And what did the Law want? Had Cousin Lucille alerted the police? Was there now a nationwide search for them?

The sound of quick footsteps prompted her to swing around.

"Paul, Paul!" Ellis shouted in high glee and raced over to her brother.

"Little girl, are you pleased to see me, or the ice-cream? No, don't bother answering!" Her brother grinned his lop-sided grin as Ellis buried her nose in the ice-cream cone. "And Eilidh, I really think if you had brains, you'd be dead dangerous. The Law was only after you because you dropped this - "

With a dramatic gesture he pulled the one-eared panda from behind his back, and Eilidh swallowed a chunk of pride. "Sis, try looking relieved, happy, grateful...." Paul's grey eyes held a good-humoured, amused twinkle as he waited for his sister's reaction.

"Yippee," she said with a not-quite smile, and got up to watch the black space widen between them and the harbour. Then she took time to admire the phosphorescence of the ship's wash and the distant horizon of cold grey-green water. She could feel the throb of the engines somewhere underneath her, while above, the gulls wheeled overhead with their raucous screams. There was a taste of salt on her lips, an unfamiliar sensation; and from the lounge drifted the sound of a strange tongue...an unknown language.

By the time they reached the island the late afternoon light had faded into the golden shades of sunset, and the three Londoners were totally exhausted. They were too tired to appreciate the parade of pastel-coloured houses sitting loftily above a harbour stacked with fishing boats, too spent to notice the total absence of kilted men. A kindly fellow passenger gave them a lift to their final destination, a small village just two miles away from the ferry terminal. The driver, an elderly lady, even knew where the house, 'Fasgadh', was situated.

"There it is" - she eventually pointed and creaked down the gears. " - up that wee hill. The name means 'shelter', and very suitable it is too, the way it nestles there among the trees. Take care and enjoy your holiday!"

With that, she deposited her passengers by the road-side. Eilidh thanked her profusely and waved her goodbye before slinging the various bags and rucksacks down on the road. Paul cradled a heavy, sticky, sleeping Elllis and looked around in awe.

Directly across the road they saw the silver-white beach stretching away to the south; the Atlantic Ocean stretching out to the endless east, and in the foreground, a spray of glimmering white foam floated lazily on to the sand. Behind them, the sun went down. The sky's colours, reflected by the sea, went from orange to the salmon-coloured rifts of sunset, sweeping great streaks of brightness across the ocean distances. The smell of the sea pervaded the air and the only sound was the slapping of water against nearby rocks.

For just a few seconds, Eilidh allowed herself to believe that only a Creator God could put on such a lavish, measureless show of colour and beauty. There had to be a Creator mind behind all this, she admitted. But she was like a blind person, who had been given sight for about two minutes, then had to go back to blindness.

"Well, what d'you think, sis?" Paul asked. "I guess this must be the edge of the world, huh? And boy, it's just got to be the sum of all our fantasies! But - is it going to be our safe haven?"

"I don't know, Paul," she said softly, thinking out loud, thinking out the words of a song. "But, if I still believed in a heaven, then...then I'd say this must be the nearest thing to heaven on this earth."

CHAPTER 4

"If you knock on that door once more, Eilidh, I'll SCREAM," Paul said tensely as they waited outside 'Fasgadh'. "Let's face it - this place is deserted. I've seen livelier looking graveyards."

As he spoke, Eilidh gave a shiver of cold and apprehension. The evening air had grown chilly. A little bird chirped scoldingly above the huge double garage and she wanted to shout at it. 'Shut up! Get lost! I'm trying to think!' Instead, she clamped a hand over her mouth to hold back the sob rising in her throat. Tears filmed her eyes as she stepped away from the front porch and looked again at the beautiful, newly-built house. It gave a blank, silent face in return. The louvre blinds were completely closed at each large window, the solid oak door mute, the sweeping lawn perfect. There were no bits of nonsense lying around. Nothing to say - the person who lives here has a wife, children, pets.

Strident, random thoughts wheeled and crashed inside her head, like disordered bees. Where would they spend the night? And the next day? And the next? Two difficult tears found their way down her cheeks.

"Oh, be a man and don't bubble," Paul called out. He hadn't intended it to be funny, but she suddenly laughed as if he'd made the joke of the century.

"I guess I've just reached the end of my rope," she said, and her words were as shaky as a lamb on newborn legs. "What do we do now? Have we come 700 miles just on a wild goose chase? Was it all for nothing?"

She sat down beside him on the wooden garden seat. She reached out, put her hand on his own, looked into his face. Five minutes separated them at birth, and they were now fifteen years down the tracks together, and he was her father, mother, brother, friend. Now she felt she had failed him.

"It's okay, sis. We're a bit hard-up on hope at the moment, but let's give positive thinking a go." Ignoring his little sister's undignified snores, he continued; his facial language proclaiming that he could deal with anything. "This place is well-kept, and you said that there's a few greenhouses at the back with stuff growing in them, and there's land over there that's obviously newly churned over - "

"So - the Paterson guy could have dropped dead with overwork!" Eilidh said the words carelessly, but the events of the last few days had worked their way through her subconscious, and had re-surfaced to haunt her.

Paul rose, still holding Ellis, and paced to the front gate. Almost absently, he stared down at the nearest house. Finally he said, without turning round, "I'll take Ellis to that house over there, see if they know anything. And there's two guys messing about with a car engine over there - see what you can suss out from them."

Propelled by some robotic impulse, Eilidh obeyed. A little golden slice of moon was in its rising, but there was still day-light colour in the land. Watery pale colour, strengthened with gold. 'Weird, it'll be totally dark in London right now,' she reflected as she neared the two figures.

The two men were tinkering with car's innards, but stopped and straightened up as she approached. One man was older, perhaps in his fifties, with a shock of silver hair, and a face well-grooved with frown lines. He was not frowning now. The younger man was in his late teens, Eilidh decided as she said, "Hi!" His tall and skinny build was compensated for by a face that could have graced an album cover.

The smile he gave her was as wide as any toothpaste ad, and for a moment, Eilidh felt a spark of joy. "Hallo!" he said. "Where did you spring from? I'm Ronnie Macpherson, by the way." He held out his hand to shake hers, but then changed his mind. "Oh-oh, we'd better not. Just because I enjoy wallowing in grease...."

She smiled, enjoying his lingering stare. A slight breeze teased her long hair and ran fingers through her white cotton jacket. "Right! I feel sticky enough after travelling - "

"Ah-hah. Is that a London accent I hear?" the older man said. He must be Ronnie's father, Eilidh decided.

"Yes! I'm not so clever with your accent, though," she admitted. "Now, if I heard you speak in London, I would have taken you for Irish."

"And you wouldn't be the first to do that," Ronnie smiled down at her. "Are you here on holiday?"

The smile made her heart skid. "No - I mean, yes, sort of. My brother and I are looking for...uh...an old friend of the family. Haven't actually found him yet!"

"Oh? Well, look no further!" Ronnie, laying down his spanner, was practically airborne with eagerness to help out. "My father knows everyone in these parts, don't you, dad?" and his father nodded vigorously in agreement.

"It's a John Paterson."

For a moment, the expression of the two men froze as if the HOLD button of a video machine had been pressed.

"W-what's wrong?" Eilidh asked, dumbfounded at the reaction. She tried to disguise the onrush of alarming thoughts and doubts that their non-verbal message had triggered off. Her voice was calm as she asked, "He's not dead, is he?"

Ronnie looked down at the ground to avoid her eyes. The older man turned away and started fiddling with cables in the engine, but not before Eilidh could see the look of hatred stamped on his face, and not before she could hear the muttered words, "No...more's the pity." And Eilidh became acutely aware of the anger that spread out from the man's hunched back and tense muscles. Could anger be that - visible? she wondered.

Silence enveloped them. From the distance came the muted hiss of the waves, and then, Paul shouting like a demented banshee, "Eilidh! Eil-idh!" She pivoted round on her heels, not wanting her face to give anything away, even though she wasn't sure whether it was fury or curiosity that her face could keep secret.

Tossing "Thanks" frostily over her shoulder, she walked away, with her chin a fraction more tilted than usual. After walking several yards, she couldn't resist a quick backward glance. Even in the now shadowy light, Eilidh got the distinct impression that son was bawling

father out. 'World-class weird' she labelled the men and
quickened her pace.

"Aw, come on! Get a move on." Paul said as she
reached him. It was his male chauvinist voice. The one
that tried to tell her what to do. And then, "You weren't
approached by the aliens, en route to the Mechanical
Men, were you? You look as if you've been hit by a
sledgehammer."

Eilidh responded with variations on the evil eye, but
Paul didn't bother to follow that look through. He was
almost holding his breath with excitement as he pulled her
along, through a wooden gate, up a shingle path, and right
up to a weather-withstanding door. "Come and meet
Mary Somebody-or-other. She's nosey, but nice, and
she's promised us a bed for the night - or at least till our
John Paterson comes out of hospital. "S'okay," he said,
noticing his sister's questioning look, "it's only a minor
op and he should be out in a couple of days. Who cares,
anyway? Who cares where we sleep? Right now, all I'm
interested in is food, glorious food!"

Warning him with, "Don't disgrace me by eating too
much," Eilidh allowed herself to be led into the warmth
and welcome of the large crofthouse. Mrs Somebody-or-
other turned out to be a Mrs Murray, a maternal, red-
haired woman who wore the remnants of a former beauty
very well. Her words were buttered with the soft island
accent.

"Come in, dear. Here, sit down, take off your jacket.
You must be exhausted! I'm sure you envy little Ellis -
look at her, wee mite, dead to the world. She didn't stir
even when her big brother laid her down on the sofa."

Warmth was spreading out from the black solid-fuel stove and Eilidh realised how cold she had been. "I didn't know how cold and tired and hungry I was" she said, shrugging off her jacket. "It's very good of you, Mrs Murray. Taking in strangers from the cold type-of-thing, you know? I don't think we'd do that for anyone back in London!"

"We wouldn't even give them a 'hello'," Paul joined in. "Where we stay, you can walk past the same people a million times and never exchange a word."

"But that's a different world altogether, isn't it?" Mrs Murray said as she pulled the chintz curtains closed against the pallor-struck darkness. Turning round, she motioned for Paul and Eilidh to pull their chairs up close to the table. "Or maybe you prefer the city life?" she asked.

Paul, flopping down in the chair, leaned his elbows on the table and rested his chin on the palm of a hand, thinking, balancing out city versus country. Right here, right now, talking about London was like talking about a different planet. "City life is okay if you're not poor, I guess. If you don't HAVE to live in some human filing cabinet like we did - uh, like we do. But then again - " He watched while Mrs Murray produced place mats, silver cutlery, tinkling china, and set them methodically on the table. " - I kinda like the way there's so much life packed into such a small area, y'know? Street noises, the sound of sirens in the distance, bright lights, takeaways, people everywhere."

'Yeah, sure,' Eilidh answered in her head, 'people everywhere, empty faces, empty eyes. No trees, no grass, no flowers, no nothing. No, that wasn't fair - ' she decided, giving herself a mental shake, getting her mind working back on all the different flats on their estate, hundreds of them. Sometimes she had wondered what was within each 'box', all the different lives lived out, and all the different small ambitions behind each life. So, there was a lot of things she could say about city life. But all she said was, "THIS is a good place for bringing up a family, I guess. Have you any children, Mrs Murray?"

"We have," Mrs Murray's smile looked proud. "We've got a wee girl and she'll be so thrilled when she wakes up to find a new friend! And you'll have to meet our other daughter, Anna. She's seventeen."

A lightbulb went on behind Paul's eyes. He had only recently discovered girls, or rather, they had discovered him. With his highly expressive face, accented with dark eyebrows and riveting grey eyes, even Eilidh thought he was handsomely thrown together. But she would have died rather than let him know that, of course.

All his smiles dried up, however, as Mrs Murray left the room and her older daughter came in to introduce herself. Gawky, plain...these were the adjectives which sprang into Eilidh's head. They were certainly appropriate. Between steel-rimmed spectacles, gold braces on her teeth, red hair scraped severely back and dowdy clothes, Anna didn't appear to have discovered her full potential.

A look of admiration washed over the girl's face as she exchanged politenesses with Paul. She was oblivious to the presence of Eilidh, who was, in any case, used to this treatment from besotted girls.

"This is my 'significant other'", Paul finally gestured

towards Eilidh, "apart from my girlfriend, that is." That
last comment earned him an under-table kick from Eilidh,
while Anna smiled palely and stammered "Oh! ...h-hallo,
Eilidh. 'Scuse me, I've got to help mum." With that, she
scurried out of the room.

"What was that for?" Paul moaned, rubbing his
ankle.

"As if you didn't know, Pinnochio!" Eilidh clarified.
"Your nose has shot out several inches!"

"But why give her the wrong impression?" Despite
Paul's efforts not to laugh, submerged gusts still found
their way to the surface as he continued, "I thought you
were on my side!"

"Shows how bright you are!" Eilidh rolled her eyes
upward. "Okay, so maybe she's not eligible for Miss
World and her clothes are from the land that style forgot,
but I'll bet she's got a lot of other redeeming features...
and we're their guests!"

"Okay, okay." Paul sobered to an elaborate caricature
of humility. "I shouldn't have made it so obvious.
Apology good enough for you?" He did his best to speak
respectfully as Mrs Murray brought in the tea things, but
an irrepressible twinkle in his eye betrayed him.

For the next ten minutes the only sounds in the room
were cutlery clinking on china, tea being swallowed,
"Mmm" from Paul and "More?" from Anna and her
mother, both of whom were playing hostess to the hilt.
Paul was delighted to be fussed over in this way. He had
always longed for a return of the days when men were men
and women knew their place.

"What's John Paterson like?" he asked, filling his

mouth with floury scone and trying to talk round it.

"Well, since he's an old family friend, you'll know more about him than we do. Of course, you won't know what he looks like - you've never actually met him, have you?" Mrs Murray said. Paul shook his head, and she went on, "What can I tell you? Let's see...he's fiftyish, a bachelor, tall and sort of distinguished looking. Although he was born and brought up in this village, he emigrated to the States after...well, when he was still a teenager. And he never came back all that time. Built up a prosperous gardening business for himself near Vermont - that much, I know!"

She watched with amusement as Paul continued to stow away food like some street urchin, then continued, "He came back here two years ago and built that beautiful big house on his father's land. I think he enjoys making things grow and, well, just being alone - "

There was a hint of mischief on Anna's face as she slotted in her own comment. "What Mum would actually like to say - " she smiled at Paul in a flash of golden bands - "is that John Paterson is dour, unfriendly, and lives the life of a hermit!"

"Oh, that explains it!" Eilidh exclaimed in a loud voice which startled them all. There was only the slightest hesitation before she added with a certain firmness. "But it doesn't excuse it, definitely not."

"Excuse what?" Anna asked.

"C'mon, Eilidh, say something else - the silence is deafening," Paul urged. He had never learnt the rules of correct behaviour in company.

His sister shook her head, impatient with the now alert,

listening silence. "The guys who were working on the car - the Macpherson's - they were a bit troubled when I mentioned John - ."

"Did...did they SAY anything?" Mrs Murray broke in, her eyes fixed on Eilidh.

Eilidh tried to smooth the situation. "Nothing, really. Must have been my imagination doing overtime!" She stifled the yawn that stretched her jaw muscles. "Gosh, I'm really whacked! If you don't mind, I'll try Ellis on the toilet and change her for bed."

"Well," Mrs Murray studied Eilidh admiringly, "you both take such good care of your wee sister. No wonder your parents can trust you with taking her on holiday." Eilidh got up from the table quickly to hide her embarassment while Mrs Murray continued. "Anna, you could never cope like that - I mean, could you really?"

"I'm sure she could, Mrs Murray...given the chance." Eilidh felt oddly good to see Anna's grateful grin, but then she turned to Mrs Murray with what she hoped was a friendly, reassuring smile. "I'm sorry! Did that sound rude? I didn't mean to, really."

"It's all right, Eilidh," Mrs Murray smiled, and began to stack the dirty dishes. "I think you may have a point there, actually. But listen, off you go to bed, have a good long lie tomorrow, and when you're ready we'll drive over to the hospital."

They all exchanged a round of 'goodnights', then Eilidh went upstairs, attended to Ellis, and got ready for bed. Sleep hung on her eyelids and pulled at her shoulders, but her mind was automatically clicking through the pattern of the day's events. Everything had gone rather well, so why was she so bitter? Was it the glimpse of the normal, humdrum home life of the Murray's? How safe and solid Anna's world was, Eilidh thought, while her own amounted to paper castles!

Lying there, in the girly-pink bedroom, she could listen to the sounds drifting up from downstairs; family talk, and a mother pottering about, fixing things for her family. Lying there, and listening, Eilidh got hungry for the ordinariness of family life.

CHAPTER 5

"Boy, do I hate hospitals!" Paul said to Eilidh the next afternoon as they waited outside the hospital's Surgical Department. There was a clean smell in the place, but not fresh clean.

"Me, too," Eilidh answered, making a puckery face.

"Reminds me of Mum and...remember that day when -."

"Oh, don't," Eilidh cut him off, closing her eyes. For Eilidh, all things to do with her mother, and her pain, had been banished away somewhere irretrievable, somewhere beyond all echoes, where the past lost the power to hurt.

"Why not? Why can't we talk about her?" There was a sheathed anger in Paul's voice as he faced her squarely. "That's the best cop-out I can think of. Just forget about her, pretend she never existed. Is that what you want, huh? Don't you care?"

Eilidh bowed her head. She answered, after a moment, and with no particular inflection in her voice, "Paul, accuse me of anything you like, but don't accuse me of not caring. Got it?"

For a minute he stared angrily at her, seeing that flat, holding-in expression she had worn since the day their mother died. Knowing that she was unmistakably serious about closing the subject, he spread out his hands in an open gesture and summoned a smile of huge cheerfulness. "Okay, okay, I'll hold the lectures. Put a smile on, sis - you're desperate to make a good impression on this guy, aren't you? Mind you, I think you've overdone it - scraping your hair back a la Anna and that fussy frilly blouse. Are you aiming to look like a leftover from the 19th Century, or what?"

"Yes, yes, yes - very amusing. Paul, this man's our last hope. We've GOT to make a good impression on him."

"Why bother?" Paul said rudely, sourness curling around the edges of his voice. "From what these mechanics said to you, and from what Mrs Murray said...well, our future doesn't look too rosy. Let's face it, the last thing this John Paterson will want in his life is one talkative tot...and two troublesome teenagers."

Eilidh, clasping her hands together, was filled with an internal shaking. She bit her lips, and looked at the approaching nurse with her eyes issuing a mute appeal. "Uh, excuse me, we came to see a Mr John Paterson," she stammered. "Is he...uh...fit for visitors?"

"Visitors for John Paterson?" The nurse, soft looking and sweet, with a white cap perched on her fair hair, smiled in surprise. "Why, that's nice! Only - "

"Is there some problem?" Paul asked.

The nurse quickly bridged the tense moment when she answered in a cheerful voice, "No! It's just that John Paterson had requested we put up a 'No Visitors' sign on the door. Not that he had any visitors, now that I think of it...oh, on you go, shock him!" she finished on a teasing note, raising a brow. "Room 7, to the left."

They thanked the nurse and followed her directions. The door of Room 7 was slightly ajar.

"Can't believe how nervous I am!" Eilidh whispered.

"Take deep breaths," Paul advised, and tapped the door gently. There was no reply and they stepped cautiously into the side room. In bed, a man lay deeply asleep.

Eilidh crept over to the bed and looked down into the sleeping face. She studied the bristling eyebrows, the dark hair with its faint sprinkling of silver, the square jaw that gave the handsome face a look of substance, of strength.

All at once, his eyes snapped open. They were blue, but very dark. "Eilidh!" His voice cracked wide open on the word, and Eilidh gulped and took a backward step. For one moment the man looked like some stricken wild creature, trapped. Beads of sweat appeared on his forehead and all colour drained from his face. His head flopped to one side on the pillows.

"W-what's wrong with him? Oh, Paul, what have we done?" Eilidh's voice came out as a squeak, just as the man opened his eyes again and asked for some water.

Eilidh held the glass of water to his lips and he took a few sips. Clattering the glass nervously down on the table, she felt her face grow hot. What was she supposed to say? She turned to stare at her brother and he stared at her and a thick silence lay all over the room.

Paul made himself sit down on the radiator. He jammed his hands down into the pockets of his jacket and stretched his long legs out in front of him. He cast his eyes down, then cast them up again. "Uh ...sorry we made you faint, Mr Paterson. I'm Paul Alexander, and this is my twin sister...but you already know her name - ."

"Her name? Of course I don't know her name!" John Paterson interrupted in his transatlantic accent, his eyes riveted to Eilidh's face. "How could I? I've never seen either of you before."

Paul shut his mouth. Then he took a deep breath and opened it again. "My mother - that is, our mother - died last week. She left a letter addressed to you. We would have posted it but - " he exchanged a quick glance with Eilidh and rushed out the words, "but the people who were supposed to look after us wanted to break us up as a family and - ."

"We have a three year old sister, too," Eilidh cut in. "Ellis."

"And we decided...to look you up," Paul finished. A vaguely embarrassed smile, which didn't register in his eyes, touched his mouth. He watched as Eilidh silently handed John Paterson the letter.

He took a full ten minutes to read the few lines. I can't stand it, Eilidh thought, her nervousness becoming unmanageable. I can't stand this waiting, this silence. It shouldn't be like this. He should say something.

"Mmm, I..." John Paterson began. Then he closed his lips over whatever else he might have wanted to say and waited, considering them both. A long, slow moment crawled by before he spoke again. When he did speak it was with deliberation, choosing each word like a lawyer. "Your mother seems to have made arrangements for me to be your guardian. I'm willing. Is that what YOU want?"

For several seconds the words did not have meaning. They were only sounds. Then Eilidh realized what he had said and shyness shortened her reply. "Yes." And then, "yes, if it's our only hope of staying together as a family."

Leaning forward in the bed, John Paterson pressed the hand bell and a red light, the size of a button, flashed on the wall panel above his bed. They could hear its persistent ring echoing down the corridor. "Pass me my dressing gown. It's on the hook - there." With these words, he swung his legs stiffly out of bed and slipped into the dark velour gown.

A nurse stepped briskly into the room. "Could you bring me my clothes, please," John Paterson said to her, "and a self-discharge form - is that what you call it? I'm going home."

CHAPTER 6

The nurse stared at John Paterson, her eyes widening in disbelief. "But - you can't! Not for another few days. I know it was just a hernia op...but, Mr Paterson, let's not be stubborn, let's be sensible - " The cool professional manner was slipping.

"Let's get my clothes, please. You looked after me well, and if it'll make you feel any happier, once I'm home, call in my doctor and district nurse and the world and his wife. But I'm going." As a thank you from a grateful patient it left a lot to be desired.

The nurse didn't know when to stop trying. "But the surgeon said - ."

"I have just been struck stone deaf," John Paterson cut in, "and I won't be able to hear even one more word on the subject." He pushed his lips together because, for him, the discussion was now closed.

The nurse flounced out of the room and Eilidh turned to John Paterson. She could feel her eyes burning up at him. She wanted to ask - why? You don't even KNOW us! Why are you doing this? And, she argued silently, you couldn't say - what's in it for you, Mr Paterson? Could she? Then she realised he was asking her a question. "...and how did you get here today?"

"Your next-door neighbour, Mrs Murray, drove us here today. She's waiting outside. We left Ellis with Anna and little Mary." A frown creased John Paterson's face. Eilidh's voice tapered off, then ceased.

"Did she ask you - what brought you here?" he asked. For a second it looked as if the frown might turn into anger, and then he almost smiled. "Knowing Mrs Murray, she'd have given you the Third Degree!"

"She did show a bit of idle curiosity," Eilidh answered with care.

"Active curiosity, I'd have said," Paul corrected her. "Don't worry, Mr Paterson, we used evasive tactics! Told her we were looking up an old friend of the family," he looked at his sister with glances out of the side of his eyes, as if he was unsure what to say next.

The question he then asked held a high-risk factor. "What WERE we supposed to say? What ARE we to think?"

"Exactly what you said." The older man winced as he struggled his feet into slippers. "'A family friend' - that's all anyone needs to know. And that 'anyone' includes you."

The twins were prevented from replying by the re-appearance of the nurse. The formalities of signing the discharge form over, she handed him his clothes, medication and a letter which had arrived for him that day. "Take good care of him now," she told the twins, "and make sure he doesn't do any heavy lifting and gets plenty of rest."

In the car, Mrs Murray listened with wide-eyed surprise as Paul launched into the edited version of events, this

time including the facts of their mother's death.   Mr
Paterson said nothing apart from, "Fine, thank you." He
stared, frowning, at the speeding landscape of the wild
and lovely land, obviously not wanting to open any
conversation, not wanting to hear what Mrs Murray
might ask.

Mrs Murray's curiosity was nowhere near satisfied by
the time they reached the silver sands beside the village.
The light in the sky and sea today was a secret shining,
with a flying patch of sun. The sea was blue, or blue-
green, and breaking loudly white. Through the open car
window they could hear its long sigh as it came far up the
beach, the soft draw on the pebbles, and then, further out,
the everlasting roar of water on rock, element against
element until eternity.

John Paterson emerged slowly and awkwardly out of
the car and handed Mrs Murray a bundle of notes. Mrs
Murray protested, "No and no and no! Please just let me
do this one neighbourly thing for you." She tried to hand
the money back but her neighbour clasped his hands
behind his back and said firmly, "Then please give it to
Anna. Paul and Eilidh really appreciate her offering to
look after their little sister today. She can buy dresses or
something...don't teenage girls always need dresses?"

"Not since the nineteen sixties," Eilidh chipped in.

Ignoring this attempt at humour, their future guardian
led the twins up the long driveway leading to the house,
through the richly-panelled hall and into the lounge. The
one room was almost as big as their entire London flat,
with none of its ragtag decor. Instead it was tastefully
decorated, and furnished with quality pieces made of

beautiful wood polished to a mellow gleam. A thick wool carpet stretching from wall to wall and chintz-covered sofas and chairs gave the room a luxurious feel.

But not a homely feel, Eilidh decided as she revolved slowly in the middle of the room, taking it all in. No unnecessary frivolities here. No ornaments, photographs, prints or plants. Just a room plucked from an Ideal Home Exhibition.

"Put a match to the fire, Paul," John Paterson said, interrupting her thoughts. "It's already set with firelighters and paper and wood. And the oil heating will come on soon."

There was a faint whoosh as the sticks and paper ignited and flames leapt up the chimney. "Wow, a real fire!" Paul said, and let the firelight wash over his face. He paused, spread his hands. "Better than that smoky paraffin heater we had in the flat. And the rooms are so big - !"

"Have a good look round while I rest here," John Paterson said. "The smaller bedroom at the end of the hall can be yours, Paul." And, turning to Eilidh, "the big room upstairs with the two single beds will do for you and ...um...Ellis? There's bedclothes in the linen cupboard and, let me see.... Oh, yes, take milk and bread out of the freezer and whatever you want for dinner. There's a microwave for defrosting." He gingerly moved into a lying position on the huge sink-down sofa, crossing his hands behind his head. The twins got the message and left the room.

A few hours later he surfaced and, looking slightly less pale and tired, turned his attention to Ellis, who had put

in an appearance while he was asleep. She was trying
very hard not to stare at the stranger. "Hallo, little girl,"
he said, trying to slip down out of adult world and come
into hers. "I'm John, and I'm going to look after you. I've
been to hospital - that's why I've been resting, you see."

Ellis stared. John Paterson attempted a half-smile. He
looked into the little face that was made for laughing, the
freckles drifting across the tilted nose, then down to the
hands that were still sticky despite the licking and wiping
on her dress.

"Op-sital!" Her huge eyes shone hopefully. "Did
you see my mummy there?"

Paul lifted his head up from his task of putting peats
on the fire. Exchanging glances with Eilidh, he muttered
"We'll have to tell her."

Eilidh moved away and sat down at the table. Telling
Ellis now loomed huge and unavoidable, but she couldn't
do it. To speak of it would, she knew, be to give it
recognition, and that in turn would make it sharp and clear
and real.

"I'm losing my mummy!" the little voice bleated,
when no one would give her an answer.

"Losing your - " Paul repeated, mystified. A few
seconds silence was followed by a glimmer of understanding. "Oh, you mean, you're missing mummy! Is that
right, sweetheart?" Ellis nodded solemnly, and Paul
reached out for a tissue from a nearby box and honked
loudly into it.

For a piercing instant, Eilidh longed to be somewhere
else. Paul squatted down beside Ellis and grasped her by
the shoulders. "Ellis...we won't see mummy again. She

died." His hands moved nervously. His eyes flickered to
Eilidh, then to John Paterson and back to Ellis. "Mummy
is now in heaven, with Jesus. Heaven is a beautiful city
of gold, Ellis, and mummy is not sick there. She's
perfectly well...and very happy." He whispered the last
words.

Puzzlement flickered in the little girl's eyes. A
measureless space of time seemed to pass before she
nodded, and moved over to the bright fire. She had never
seen an open fire before, and knelt before it in awe,
allowing the light and shadows to move across her face.

Paul and Eilidh stared at each other through the heavy
quietude that filled the room. There seemed nothing else
they could possibly say. Should they now allow the
person of their mother to become a mere footnote in their
sister's memory, Eilidh asked herself; or should they
work hard to keep that memory, that presence alive?
Should they speak of the anxieties of the living years, or
the peace of the dying hours? At last, John Paterson broke
the silence. He kept his face closed off as he said "So your
mother was a Christian, then?"

"Uh-huh. Well, she became one just before she died.
She taught Ellis a little prayer and - " Paul slipped his eye
over to where Eilidh was sitting, " - she asked us to read
the Bible every day. 'Don't forget...to remember the
Bible.' Wasn't that the way she said it, Eilidh?"

"Something like that," she agreed. "Sometimes it
was hard to make out the words."

John nodded, then said, "And do you?"

"What - read the Bible?" Paul said. "No. I suppose we
should, because it's the last thing Mum did say to us but - ."

"We no longer believe." Eilidh's voice sounded certain.

"Oh. I see." John Paterson stood up slowly and walked over to the leaded windows where he watched the birds sing their April song. "I don't actually have a Bible, but we'll get one first thing. And we'll read it together, just like your mum wanted." He turned to look at them. "Just because YOU don't believe, you shouldn't deprive Ellis of being brought up in the way your mum thought was important. I mean - " he screwed up his face in thought, staring up to the ceiling, then added, to no one in particular, "I suppose it could be argued that it's impossible for anyone to intelligently, reject -or accept - God without ever really having a chance to know anything about him. Am I right? That there is no real, no true freedom without, first of all, a knowledge of the choices?"

Paul stood frowning, considering the complexity of it all. "I suppose not," he said in a tone which didn't match his words, but Eilidh just pursed her lips tightly together, sealing up the negative response. Like, she HAD known about God, but all that praying, well, it had only proved to be wasted emotion, hadn't it?

"Now, if I'm going to look after you," John Paterson said, bringing her back to the present, "I'd better do some phone calls. Your mother's vicar, and then your cousin - what was her name again? - Lucille. Tomorrow I'll send for your school and medical records...family allowance book...that sort of thing." He swallowed back a yawn and moved away from the window. A sudden pain must have overtaken him because he grimaced and held his side. The veins on his forehead stood out blue against the white of his face, and he murmured "Get my Distalgesics, Paul.

They're in my jacket pocket."

Paul quickly fetched the tablets and a drink of water, but Eilidh said in exasperation, "Stubborn, that's what the nurse said, isn't it? And she was a hundred per cent right. You should have stayed in hospital and made a proper recovery. What use are you to us if you...you -" she stopped when she heard the anger in her own voice, and felt the old, clutching fear return. Scooping up Ellis into her arms, she hurried out the door, letting it slam behind her.

While she was still marching down the hall, she heard the door opening behind her, and through it Paul's disembodied voice. Eilidh just stood there, flat against the wall, her mouth open, listening to the words. " - look, it's okay, just leave her. Eilidh's been bitter since mum died. We've got this far, and we're safe, together, at last. But now she probably feels threatened again, because you look like death warmed up! D'you get that? I mean, can you understand that?" Eilidh didn't wait for John Paterson's reply. She knew that any expression of negative feelings would tip her back over to being afraid, being insecure. At the same time, when she thought over how melodramatic she must have sounded, she felt the need to laugh hysterically.

Despite her sister's weight, Eilidh took the stairs two or three at a time, leaping catlike up to the room that was all light and airy and unlived in. Once lying on the uncreased bed, she covered her face with her hands as if to blot out what she had said. Ellis sucked her thumb and sat the time through until she fell asleep.

CHAPTER 7

Over the week that followed, John Paterson did heed the various health warnings he had received. He rested every day and submitted himself to the attentions of the District Nurse and G.P. Soon the stitches were removed from his wound, and his colour and energy levels improved.

April became May. The Alexander family were settling in just as spring was settling in. Eilidh had never seen the seasons unfold like this before, because all she had really known was the concrete jungle of the inner city. And now, here she was right amongst things that were growing, changing, moving. The birds were all singing like crazy creatures, because it was springtime, and the wild daffodils were flowering and everything out of doors smelt clean, new, and fresh. The air itself seemed to tingle with promise and Eilidh began to feel the same as the birds, young and alive and free.

"Every day here seems to be the kind of day you just want to rush out and meet," she commented one afternoon as the sun slid through the kitchen windows. "Ellis would need to be tethered to keep her indoors these days."

"I thought you city folk would find this place boring." John Paterson said. To his tea-cup, not to Eilidh.

Why can't he look me straight in the eye, for once?

Eilidh wondered, while admitting to herself that he didn't seem to have the same problem with her siblings. "Ellis!" she said aloud, as her sister came racing towards them like a bus with its brakes off. "Is that flower for me?"

"No - for John!" Ellis laughed, infecting them all with her vitality. She handed him the ghost of a bluebell which her grasp had taken, together with a severed root and a random handful of grasses. She held out her love to them all, giving it to them. "Please, John, can I want - "

"Can I HAVE," John Paterson corrected her gently.

"Can I have a pet lamb? Her mummy can't feed her and I can...please? Please!"

"Typical female!" Paul said with a derisive snort. He leant over the kitchen table, scooping up stray grasses. "Turns the charm full on, then - wham - in with the request! And we males fall for the act like true suckers!"

"Thank you, little girl," John Paterson said, permitting Ellis a rare smile and admiring her flower. "Now, are you looking after that kitten I let you keep? I see little Tiger's been busy sharpening her claws on the furniture!" Ellis beamed with pleasure at this compliment as he went on, "and I'll only let you keep a lamb if I'm sure you'll look after it well."

Ellis loudly catalogued all she was doing for the kitten, which, in her excitement, she was calling Lion. Meanwhile, Eilidh teased out Paul's last words. "'We males fall for the act like true suckers.' I've got to hand it to you, Paul. This is definitely one of your better exaggerations!"

"What d'you mean, sis?" Paul asked innocently. His teeth had a piratical flash, his grey eyes twinkling and penetrating.

"You know! Anna's been making cow-eyes at you all week. Her I.Q. seems to drop to zero when you appear on the scene and - "

Paul drew himself up a little straighter, saying hotly, "Oh, c'mon, don't try and lay a guilt trip on me!"

"Her only request, I think, is that you look her way, and what does she get every time? The cold shoulder. Right?"

"Please!" John Paterson cut them off warningly. "You've been through this argument at least nine hundred and ninety nine times already...and Paul, turn that noise down, please!"

"Noise? You mean...but that's the new No. 1!"

"Then a whole generation needs their brains scanned," the older man said dryly. "Down, please!"

As Eilidh turned round to lower the volume, her hip caught the table, crockery chinked and a tumbler committed suicide off the edge, splattering orange juice up the kitchen units. "Oh, I don't believe this!" she whispered, looking as if she was wishing a hole would suddenly appear for her to drop down into.

"It's all right, no harm done," John Paterson said quietly, reaching out for the dishcloth.

"It's not all right!" Was that alien, raucous voice her own? "Why d'you treat me differently anyway...scared to give me a row, or something? And I'll clean it up myself, okay?"

The silence was so acute that a pin dropping onto the luxury cushion floor would have been heard a mile away. Paul, who normally would never have been credited with tact, defused the potentially explosive situation with the deftness of a bomb disposal officer.

"It's these female hormones," he said to John Paterson
in a stage-whisper, "they can be a downright nuisance,
y'know?" With that, he proceeded to mop up the mess
with kitchen towels. Eilidh almost laughed out loud at this
male chauvinist piglet that was her brother, but stopped
as she realised that John Paterson had taken a hesitant step
towards her, seemed to think better of it, and stepped
back. Instead of speaking to her, he turned to her sister
saying, "all right, Ellis, I'll probably live to regret it, but,
yes, you can have a lamb. We'll check with Mr Murray
first, and then I'll teach you how to give her the bottle."

"Like a baby?" Ellis clapped her hands.

"Yes, like a baby. In fact - shh!" He held a warning
finger to his lips, "I think that's Anna's footsteps."

It was, and as Anna walked in to a rapturously noisy
welcome from Ellis, Eilidh understood, right then, just what
they done to this remote and solitary man. She saw in a flash,
but for always, the totality of their intrusion into John
Paterson's life. But she tucked away those thoughts for later
on, and concentrated on making Anna feel welcome.

Paul slammed around the kitchen, making coffee for all.
Eilidh, having recovered from her minor outburst, hid an
amused smile at her brother's attempts to avoid Anna. She
turned to her new neighbour. "Anna, how d'you fancy a
day's shopping in town? We all need new clothes; Ellis is
growing fast and Paul and I need school uniform. I'd
welcome an extra pair of hands to carry all the bags."

"I'd love to! But - " Anna paused, looked at John
Paterson and then at Eilidh, "school uniform? You mean, for
school, here?"

"Yeah! We're staying here, for good. Mr Paterson - I mean John - is now our legal guardian. So we'll be starting at your school on Monday. We've missed a bit of your summer term, but I'm sure we'll catch up okay."

A smile crept over Anna's face, revealing a golden glint. "That's terrific! And, about shopping, you'll need to come too, Paul - it's hard to judge a boy's size, isn't it Eilidh?"

Eilidh felt herself fill with laughter as she watched Paul clang the kettle back on the stove and heard his wild excuses. Even John Paterson smiled his tightly controlled, muscular smile. He said, "Yes, both Eilidh and Paul are badly in need of new clothes. Look at these jeans, Paul, they're so faded - they must be quite ancient - and that jumper-type thing, it's a few sizes too big for you, isn't it?"

Paul looked shocked. "Too right, it is - it's meant to be! And," - he flicked his hands downwards - "these jeans, man, they're NEW!"

John coughed apologetically and, after a moment's awkward silence, Anna said, "Oh, Mr Paterson, I forgot to give you this." She handed him an envelope, saying, "Mum found it while she was cleaning out the car - must have dropped out of your pocket the day you came from hospital."

He slit open the envelope and took out a bright and flowery Get Well card. After studying the card for a minute, he got up abruptly, sending the pine chair rocking backwards. His jaw was set, jutting, and he stormed out of the kitchen, riding the waves of some terrible anger.

They heard the slam of the dustbin lid outside and then

- nothing. Anna, her blue eyes worried, sensed the mood of the twins's silence, and invited Ellis to tea. After they left, Paul and Eilidh stayed sitting in the warm, murmuring kitchen, vibrating now with sunshine. For a while, the silence was so deep it could be felt as a tangible thing, a thing so solid it stopped Eilidh from drinking her coffee.

"Should we ask him..." she began.

"No," Paul said. "He'll just go into a none-of-your-business routine."

"What about the card? Should we - "

"No way! He'd throw a mental!"

"You're right."

Paul ate seriously, his eyes cast down. He chomped on a banana sandwich and gulped down his coffee. Then, at the same instant, they both got up and shot outside. Inside the dustbin, the card nestled amongst potato peelings and empty Coke tins.

"I don't believe this!" Paul gasped, spraying bread crumbs on the card. Over his shoulder, Eilidh looked at the words 'Get Well Soon', and the angry black capitals of DON'T immediately before. At the bottom were the words 'Do us all a favour'. It was signed 'R. Macpherson'.

Eilidh could feel their united anger bubbling up. She couldn't believe what she was reading. Paul didn't pause to re-read it, but tore down the drive and out the gate like a bulldozer. When Paul was angry, he didn't wait. Eilidh knew that. He couldn't hide his feelings and pretend everything was all right, not for one single solitary moment.

For once Eilidh didn't stop to marvel at the immense vastness of the sea under the sky, or the black rocks, and the white spume breaking over them. Instead she raced towards the Macpherson's house. Her heart was pounding and her throat felt constricted, but still, she had nearly caught up with her brother by the time he reached the house.

A slim frame appeared in the doorway. Blonde and pretty, with features drawn by a fine pen, Jean Macpherson looked almost too young to be Ronnie's mother. Definitely a decade younger than her husband, Eilidh decided as her brother asked for Ronnie's whereabouts.

"Oh, you must be the family staying with John Paterson!" Mrs Macpherson's warmth and friendliness fell over Eilidh like sunshine as she looked her way, "...and you must be Eilidh." A wide and generous smile washed over her face as she continued, oblivious to Paul's keyed-up questions. "My son wouldn't thank me for saying this, but I've watched Ronnie all week trying to bump into you! "

"It's Ronnie we've come to see," Paul said again, in a voice that tried to be carelessly casual but was as hard as steel. "Where is he?"

"Tinkering with that mechanical wreckage, I'm sure! You know, his first few days home from college, he roars around in it like a rocket. The next few weeks, it's repairs and adjustments every minute..." Her vigorous chat dried up as Paul wheeled round and scooted down the drive.

"Nice meeting you, Mrs Macpherson," Eilidh said apologetically. "Gotto go now." It took Mrs Macpherson a minute, and then her smile came back. She called out an uncertain "goodbye" as Eilidh tore off in long, sprinting strides after her brother. Down the drive, across the road, and over to where Ronnie Macpherson was working on his car.

She arrived there just in time to see Paul's swinging fist catch Ronnie on the cheek. Not like a punch in fights on television. Not with the handclap sound in a Western bar-room brawl. Just the horrible thud of knuckles against flesh. The older youth fell, and Paul, driven by his own impetus, toppled over him, and by the time he regained his feet, Ronnie had staggered into a half-standing position.

"Oh, Paul! You didn't have to do THAT - " Eilidh began with choking fury, but stopped when Ronnie stood up, drew his arm back and cracked Paul smack in the mouth.

"Oh, Ronnie, you didn't have to - ! Oh, Paul! Are you okay? Oh - DON'T!" Eilidh screamed as Paul, regaining his position, buried his fist in Ronnie's stomach. Ronnie reeled backwards, then, breathing hard, stopped to lean against the car. In a time zone that spaced out slower than slow motion, the fighting males glared at each other. It was just like one wolf recognising another, Eilidh thought.

"Okay, okay, time out guys - this is getting boring," Eilidh cried, zipping into the space between them. She decided 'if you can't join 'em, beat 'em'. "Earth-to-Paul..." she tried again, waving her hands in front of her, trying to catch the attention of her advancing brother. Anger and frustration blazed out of his every pore, as the air stayed full of ugliness.

"That'll teach you, jerk!" Paul shouted at his opponent, ignoring Eilidh's appeal.

"You never told me your brother was a lunatic, Eilidh," Ronnie sputtered, his brown eyes sparkling dangerously. Making himself stand up straight and face Paul squarely, he said, "Look, you little Cockney squirt, find yourself some other form of recreation, will you? You're not in one of your East End gangs now!"

"Wish I was! You - you're not even worth spitting on! At least THEY have a certain...code. They'd never stoop to anything as mean as - "

"As what?" Ronnie challenged, with a snap of his lips.

Eilidh, fishing the card out of the pocket of her jeans, silently walked over and handed it to him. As he read it, there was weather on his face, endless changes. He spat out something incomprehensible, probably some Gaelic gobbledegook, Eilidh thought.

"Of all the stupid things to do!" he said at last, his voice raspy.

"Wait for it - here comes the excuse," Paul goaded him with a derisive snort.

"There's no excuse. That's just the trouble! This is my father's handwriting; my father - Roderick!" Paul shot his sister an incredulous glance as Ronnie went on. "I can see why you were so mad. It's like...like kicking a dog when he's down. No. There's no excuse for that - not even in the past."

"Meaning?" Paul taunted.

Ronnie breathed out slowly. "Look, right now, my jaw's too sore to explain anything to YOU. You should've checked your facts before you used your fists." His angular and easy-moving body took a step forward. "Beat it, boyo, before I do something I'll regret. On second thoughts, I won't regret anything. Skedaddle!"

"I suppose that's what's known as an exit line," Paul said with studied nonchalance. "Anyway, I've had it to here" - he pointed to his throat - "with your island mysteries." He moved away, followed by Eilidh.

"Don't walk away angry," Ronnie's words were triumphant, "just walk away." And then, in a different tone, "Eilidh?"

Eilidh turned round to face the voice coming from behind her. Ronnie was taking a few slow steps in her direction, and she saw that his jeans were stained with grass, and an angry red line marked out his jaw. As he then stood and waited, he cocked his head to one side and allowed a half-smile to lighten his expression. "I don't suppose you - "

"No, I wouldn't. Whatever it is, I would not!" she replied. She straightened her shoulders and lifted her chin a little. They stood facing each other.

"Could we start again?" he persisted. "Turn a clean page with no mistakes on it?" He paused for a moment before he said, "Why I'm saying all this...I'm trying to apologise."

"I'm waiting to hear the words."

"I'm sorry. I'm sorry about the other night. Dad was downright rude to you and I should have said something, but .... you don't know my father. He'd have a fit if I tried to explain. So - " he stopped and continued to look at her with his steady eyes, almost probing into her mind, " - am I forgiven?"

"No."

"'No?' Now I'm asking myself - what is the girl thinking? What's going on in her head? Her eyes give me no clue. If only they could speak. C'mon, grey eyes, speak to me!" He broadened his grin and it seemed to work.

"No explanation, no forgiveness." Her eyes were smiling, but she didn't allow the rest of her face to reveal that. Silence held them. A loud silence in which she became aware of the whispering rush of the waves up the flat sandy part of the beach. Then the babyish crying of a far-away lamb. And above everything, the chatter and call of the seagulls as they soared in the air, interweaving patterns against the cloudless sky. Their melancholy sounds sank without an echo into the sea. Finally Ronnie spoke.

"I suppose, in a small village like this, you'd find out soon enough. But...I'd rather not be the one to tell you. You see, for our family, the subject is strictly taboo - my father will never, never allow us to speak about it." He stopped, took a breath, then started talking again. "And, well...it's not really fair on John Paterson either. I mean, he's not here to defend himself, is he?"

"Defend himself from what?"

There was a slow dawning on Eilidh's part as she waited for Ronnie to drag the words out, watched him as he frowned, cleared his throat, and positioned himself so that he didn't have to look at her. It dawned on her that the words he was going to say would be irrevocable. They could never be unsaid.

"My father blames him for the death of his brother. Peter.... Peter was only nine when John Paterson knocked him over with his car."

CHAPTER 8

'My father blames John Paterson for the death of his brother.'

Even now, days later, Eilidh shivered and felt the goose bumps speckle her arms as she recalled those words. Her heart lifted on a powerful wave of compassion as she watched John Paterson. He was supervising Paul as he transplanted seedlings into a cold frame. The two were close together, heads almost meeting, completely absorbed in their task. John showed Paul how to handle the seedlings as gently as if they were newly-hatched chickens, shaking out delicately their fine fibrous claws, and then setting them firmly in their new soil bed.

As she watched them, questions kept popping up in her mind; Oh, John, John - how did you survive that terrible night? Was there no one who would stick up for you? Was there no one who could share YOUR grief? Why did no one help you? She felt a mighty surge of anger rush over her. It was centred on her own powerlessness to undo that unspeakable situation that haunted John Paterson even now, decades later. She ached for this man and for all that had gone wrong in his life.

Her mind drifting backwards to that awful, damning sentence, she turned Ronnie's revelation over and over in her mind in great snatches and scenes. Ronnie's voice, '...blames John Paterson...killing...only nine.' At the time, as those words were spoken, Eilidh felt as if winter had suddenly descended and closed about her heart. Her mouth had opened. It opened and it stayed open while Ronnie continued.

'It was about, let's say, thirty six or thirty seven years ago. My father and John Paterson were teenagers, growing up in this village. John had just passed his driving test and gotten a car - everyone was madly jealous! Hardly any of the adults had a car in these days, never mind teenagers. It seems that John was also dating the local doctor's daughter, so he was having a zillion times more fun than anyone else.'

'One night in mid-summer, he was going for his girlfriend. A man in a hurry, you could say. He sped down a hill. Little Peter - my father's brother - was coming towards him on a bike. He was knocked off...and the car only stopped when it crashed in some boulders, further down the hill.'

Eilidh felt her face grow cold and she looked down at her hands. What was she supposed to say? The words 'I'm sorry' started to form themselves on her lips. Ronnie looked at her quickly, his eyes asking her to let him carry on. She did.

'The first people on the scene found John Paterson cradling the dead child in his arms. There wasn't a mark on little Peter, while John was covered in blood. He had gone through the windscreen when the car crashed, you see. When my father appeared and saw his wee brother, he went berserk - he was beside himself with grief and - .'

'Did...did he blame John? Right there and then?' Eilidh asked, in a voice that began to falter.

'No, not then,' Ronnie answered. 'Well, that's what I've been told anyway, and you can always trust the village gossip to keep you right! No, apparently he turned on John at the funeral. Wouldn't let him walk with the other mourners. When John tried to tell him something about faulty brakes, my father screamed 'Liar!' and 'Murderer!' It seems he had to be bodily held back by the other mourners.'

'Oh no, how awful.'

'Mmm. It must have been one ugly scene. John Paterson took off from that funeral and ran all the way to his girlfriend's home. But the house was deserted. The entire family had left the island. Probably didn't want to be associated with such a scandal, I suppose.'

Eilidh couldn't 'suppose', couldn't imagine - she could only stand there, and be appalled.

'It was tragic all round, Eilidh,' Ronnie said, and his voice sounded his concern for her. 'Tragic for John Paterson, because he left the island and never came back - at least, till a wee while ago. Tragic for my granny, because she blamed herself for allowing Peter on the bike that day, and she suffered from depression for the rest of her life. And tragic for my grandfather, because drink became his solace. He became a hopeless alcoholic.'

'And tragic for your father,' Eilidh added, aware that shadows were now beginning to soften the clear, bright light of day. Aware, too, that the tide was going out; it sank and sighed and dragged itself unwillingly away. She felt a little chill that was more than the late afternoon wind bearing its smell of seaweed.

Ronnie looked at her half-averted face and moved even closer beside her. 'They say he bottled it all up, refused to talk about it. Still won't. But it's obvious since John Paterson reappeared that Dad is still bitter; still has all the old anger. He's neither forgiven, nor forgotten. And I was born into that bitterness....'

"Hey, sis!" Paul's loud voice in her ear brought Eilidh back to the present. Leaning forward, he tapped her on the forehead. "Yoo-hoo - ! Anybody home - ! I'm beginning to think you've got a problem with your hearing, girl."

She laughed. "Selective deafness, Paul. I've a habit of tuning out rubbish talk." It was a relief to be back in the present and to laugh.

"Not rubbish talk this time, sis. Listen to this; John feels I should make horticulture my career. What d'you think of that?"

Automatically as clockwork, she answered, "Great! You can kiss goodbye to dreams of the dole then, can't you?" She leaned back on the wooden garden bench and laced her fingers behind her head. She looked up at the jet trails streaked across the open sky, feathery white lines slicing through the vast field of blue. And continuing in a reflective mood, she thought of the life Paul had lived in London, and the life he had now.

Right now, he was off and away talking about seedlings and soil and career prospects as if, if he didn't get it all said, it would never happen. And Eilidh realized how, over the last few years, her brother must have felt trapped in someone he didn't want to be. A trouble-maker, a rebel, a crazy from a broken home and a bad estate - everyone had kept him there, treated him as though he only fitted that particular mould. And maybe, Eilidh thought, maybe it was easier just to act the person they wanted you to be.

"There you go again, sis. You're tuning me out!"

She smiled lazily, and pushed back her dark hair, anchoring a stray strand behind one ear. "Just thinking of all the things John's been saying to you. At least, he TALKS to you. He doesn't exactly break his neck being communicative with me."

"Probably can't relate to stupid girls," Paul said cheerfully, and sprawled on the bench beside her in the pale morning light. "Speaking of stupid girls, is that Anna's voice I'm hearing?"

It was, in the distance. "Oh, yes!" Eilidh grinned.

"Oh no!"

Eilidh mimed a kiss, saying, "Oh Romeo, Romeo, Romeo...."

"Knock it off!" His face was firm, emphasising a slight cleft in his chin. "I'm telling you, she's like a virus that I can't shake off." He rearranged his limbs so that he was tensed, and ready-for-off. "I mean, I've tried to give the message that, as far as she's concerned, an early frost has settled on me. But no, there's been no correlation between my disappearing acts and her cranial capacity."

"Her what? Shhh - here she comes! Paul, remember, Anna and I going to town together, and it's not natural and healthy to keep on treating her like a lower life form.... Hi, Anna!" she greeted her neighbour, "ready to do some damage in town?"

"You bet!" Anna's eyes beamed behind the glasses and she flashed a metallic grin. Paul went into his usual

must-go routine of having some work to do, and Eilidh
felt herself begin to shake with laughter, inside, where it
didn't show to anyone.

Anna let out a gasp of exasperated air. "Tell me,
Eilidh, what's his problem? Is he a workaholic, and
desperate for his fix - or what? Honestly, he treats me as
if I was the carrier of some new treatment-proof plague!"

Eilidh's successful struggle not to laugh was nearly
strangling her, and she was relieved that John Paterson's
re-appearance prevented her from answering. Handing
Eilidh a wad of ten-pound notes, he said in a curious,
embarassed way, "Buy a Bible and some Jesus stories for
Ellis...and some knick-knacks to make our house a bit
more homely."

"Knick-knacks? You don't mean these grotty cats in
glass bowls - that type of thing?"

"How should I know? I'm only a mere male, after
all." He smiled and the long creases in his face curved and
deepened. Eilidh was beginning to notice the occasional
smile. But they usually flitted so quickly across his face,
if she wasn't watching out for them, she'd miss them
completely.

"Well, let's see...homely..." Eilidh said thoughtfully,
and John Paterson looked at her to give ideas, as if he
really cared what these ideas would be, so she went on.
"Mmm. How about brass and copper things for the
lounge, to reflect the firelight? And brass photograph
frames. I've got a neat photo of Ellis, and then, there's our
school one...and - have you any photographs?"

"I'm sure I can find one," he answered. "Or you
could have a look through the bureau yourself when you

come home. My parent's wedding photo should be there
- it's one of those starched and solemn affairs."

The talk then drifted into shopping details until John
turned his attention to Anna. "I want to give you some
money, too. Now close your mouth, Anna, it doesn't do
you justice!" He smiled a little at Anna's expression and
cocked his head. "You see, your parents have offered to
look after Ellis every morning during school-time. They're
even more stubborn than I am and won't take anything for
it. So - more clothes?"

"But you've already -" Anna stammered, but he pressed
the money firmly into her hand and strode away. She turned
to Eilidh, obviously after a lot of mental juggling, "He must
think I'm a real dowdy frump. And I wasn't going to buy
clothes. See, I'd saved for ages to buy those soft contact lens,
and I've made an appointment for them today, you know,
seeing as I was going to the dentist to get these railway tracks
off. And now, there's money to splash out on clothes as well.
Honestly, words fail me - "

"At last!"

"Oh, you!" Anna laughed, and pulled off her hair
bobble, shaking loose a tangle of badly-combed hair. A
sad little smile jumped about her lips as her eyes circled
the garden, looking for Paul. "It's just...all of a sudden,
I'm beginning to feel as ugly as Cinderella's stepsister. I
mean, look at today, Paul cleared off so fast he practically
left scorch marks on the pavement."

"Look, forget this I-hate-me-routine, Anna." Eilidh
had caught on to the despair in her neighbour's voice, and
proceeded to offer her the hairdressing appointment she
had booked for herself.

"Just wait," she finished, "Paul will be knocked for six when you come off that bus - I'll guarantee you!"

There was scurry of flashing legs, and then Ellis' sing-song disaster voice, "Here's the bus, here's the bus - and you're gonna lose it!" Eilidh and Anna ran out into that double ration of tingling light, into the breathless spaces. The day was theirs.

By the time the two shoppers arrived back home, the sun, bright and lifeless, was lowering itself wearily behind the western horizon. 'Fasgadh' no longer seemed cold and unwelcoming, Eilidh observed as they staggered, bags-laden, into the hall. The house was full of voices, full of movement, full of cooking aromas and kitchen sounds; through the open hall door drifted the salt tangy air and the murmuring wash of the waves. Home. Yes, home!

"Coo-ee - we're home!" Eilidh called, shooting a mischievous glance at the stranger beside her. "Hi, Paul...well, what d'you think?" she asked her approaching brother, and jerked an elbow in Anna's direction.

Paul's face had undergone its entire repertoire before he finally spluttered, "Wow! Gosh, Anna, you ARE a sight for sore eyes! That's a real eye-catching outfit! But where's your specs...and the braces? And the hair - it's so different. YOU'RE so different!"

Eilidh grinned and combed her own tousled hair back with her fingers. Anna's clutter-free beauty had obviously hit Paul like an explosion; the symmetry of her face, the shining cloud of auburn hair, now cut in a swinging bob, the dense lashes framing wide-spaced eyes.

Eyes which now studied Paul with something near to

sadness. "Different?" Anna asked Paul. "I'm not different. I'm still me...you know, the girl who automatically triggered off the frostbite in you?"

Her manner was a curious blend of boldness and vulnerability, and Eilidh could see that Paul was about to have one of his less frivolous moods. A hesitant smile curled around his lips and he threw his arms into the air in mock surrender. His voice was marshmallow-soft as he said, "I'm sorry."

"I'll live. Anyway, got to go." Anna jerked a discreet thumbs-up signal to Eilidh, as she tossed a casual 'Bye' over her shoulder.

"There's a lesson in that, I think!" John Paterson said from his doorway position, his bushy eyebrows raised in tolerant amusement. Just as Eilidh recognised that for once his smile occupied his face fully, it disappeared. He said seriously, "I remember hearing, long ago, that God loved us, just as we were. We didn't have to dress up, or try to impress him - he welcomed us just as we were. Not exactly like us, eh?"

Paul tried to scoop up his judgemental error with a smile. Squaring his shoulders he said, "Right! Never let it be said that I'm in for the feet-of-clay award. I'm off to repair the damage." His face settled into its tough-sort-of-handsome look, and then he took off after Anna. Eilidh, meanwhile, handed her purchases to John.

"There's the Bible, and a Bible Story book; and here's the photograph frames. I got all sorts of sizes - " Her eyes roamed around the lounge, visualising the brass frames displaying signs of family life. "And where did you say your parent's wedding photo was?"

"In the bureau drawer, I think. Thanks, Eilidh. Thanks for this," John said, running his fingers down the Bible with reverence. "We'll remember to read it tonight, and every night."

There was a kind of excitement in his voice, an alertness, and after he left to attend to the dinner, Eilidh wondered. She wondered about him, about that awful summer evening, about the everlasting bitterness that had greeted him on his return home from the States. All the love and protectiveness of her femininity was flooding out to him at that moment, as she thought that maybe the sadness was to be there forever, something to be carried around deep inside him, all the time.

The uneasiness Eilidh had felt the last few days had vanished in the laughter of their trip to town. So why then this wave of sadness, she asked herself as she rummaged through the old photos in the bureau. She studied the photos of long-dead relatives of John Paterson, the little family museum taken from another world, another time. Why wish that things can be undone, she challenged the faces smiling out at her from under glass. After all, wishes are wishes, and facts are facts, and that summer night - she stopped, and did a double-take at the photo in her hand.

It was an oldish photograph of a young man in a soldier's uniform. Hands behind his back, looking directly into the camera, a strong, high-cheekboned face, a lop-sided grin, a cleft in the chin.

Her stomach did a flip-flop as she gasped aloud "Paul! Paul? - can't be! Course not...but who on earth - ?" She flicked the faded print over and read aloud.

"John Paterson, United States Army."

CHAPTER 9

Eilidh's mind still nibbled at the photographic revelation through her first chaotic day at their new school, and now, right through the evening family worship. "You turned my wailing into dancing;" John's voice read out, "you removed my sackcloth and clothed me with joy."

Her mind's eye conjured up the photograph once again. Should she say something about her discovery? Or would she wait till John himself explained his true relationship to them? Would he ever do that? Perhaps it was something he was ashamed of, or wanted to forget...but how could he ever forget, now that they were living with him? He was reminded, daily. That recessive gene that ordained high cheek-bones, slightly cleft chin and lop-sided grin, had emerged in his - grandson? Eilidh was lost in a tangle of thought as John offered up a short, simple prayer.

The worship over, Ellis was settled into bed for the night while Paul spent a full ten minutes in front of the hall mirror combing his hair. "D'you think it's better this way?" he asked Eilidh as she passed him.

"Oh, Paul, how can you improve on perfection?"

"No need to be sarcastic, sis." he grinned impishly, adding by way of explanation, "I'm going over to Anna's - check that Ellis hasn't left her teddy over there."

Eilidh laughed out loud at this insultingly silly statement. "Oh, yeah, and the cow jumped over the moon!"
In the shorthand of their relationship she got to the point
quickly. "It's great to see you develop your manhood,
brother dear, but this U-turn with Anna - this is high
comedy."

"Am I laughing?" He stared into the mirror again,
then made a face. "Honestly, women! Can't live with
them, can't live without them!" Then the face became
serious. "Eilidh? D'you think Anna likes me?"

"Can fish swim?"

"Right! OK, see you." He grabbed his new wax
cotton jacket and disappeared outside into the glimmering
dusk.

"Honestly, how does he get into such situations?"
Eilidh asked John, who was sponging down the pine
work-tops in the kitchen.

"It sure can't be easy," he replied, twisting round to
face her. They both smiled hesitantly, then began to laugh
with growing conviction, until the warmth of shared
laughter enveloped them. For Eilidh, this was a good
moment. Finally John said, "How was school? I wanted
to ask you earlier, but I don't have a remote-control
button to turn Ellis's sound off!"

As the evening folded in over the house, they discussed
school at length. The breeze from the open window began
to wash cold over Eilidh and, getting up to close it, she
noticed that the sun still hung red, just above the horizon,
as if it were being sucked down into the sea. Before
closing the window, she turned round. "John...there were
a dozen different things coming out of my mouth just now,

but only one thing on my mind," - she barely recognised her own voice as the words came creeping out - "can I ask you something?"

"Sure, fire away."

"Are you our grandfather?"

For a while, Eilidh was only aware of the faintest sounds drifting in from outside; the voice of the sea conversing loudly in agitation to the sky, trees stirring, the lonely cry of a pee-wit. She had been so quietly-spoken herself that she almost hadn't heard her own words. She wondered if she'd really said the words or just thought them.

There was no reaction from John Paterson. Her heart took a picture of him sitting there, sitting very still. And the compassion she felt for him was almost as great as the disgust she now felt for herself. The head, bowed low over the kitchen table, blurred for a fraction of a second, but then as he began to speak, her vision became clear again.

"Yes," he said. "Yes, I am, and I was going to tell you, in time. I knew my...my past would catch up on me - I knew that." His face was serious and it was almost as if he was looking inside his own mind for the words he was going to speak. Eilidh stayed still, not to interrupt, not to distract. In any case she didn't know what to say next.

"I forgot that my army photo was in the bureau. Is that how you knew?" She nodded, mute, and he went on. "I'm sure you were stunned at the likeness between Paul and myself. But it wasn't because of Paul that I worked out who you were, that day in the hospital. I don't look like him now - grey hair and wrinkles and pouches under the eyes have seen to that! No, it wasn't Paul." There was something more on his mind, something he obviously wanted to say. Eilidh made herself stand and wait for it. "It was you."

"Me?"

"Yes, you. Not so much your general...um, appearance. You see, when I woke up to find you peering down into my face - all I saw were those eyes. My Eilidh's eyes. Dark grey, flecks of hazel in them, those tangled long lashes - no, don't look embarassed, Eilidh. I'm just telling so you'll understand why I said 'Eilidh.'"

"So you did say it! But...my auntie's name - sorry, my grandmother's name - was Helen."

He nodded, then brought a hand up to his face to hide the tears welling in his eyes. "I called your grandmother 'Eilidh'. It was a sort of pet name, a private name. 'Eilidh' is the Gaelic for Helen, you see."

Between each statement he hesitated, as if to be sure he was properly understood. "When you told me your name, and that your mother's name was Joan, it was a sign to me that Eilidh never forgot me, in the same way that I never forgot her."

He inhaled audibly as he sat back in the chair, but Eilidh stood unmoving beside the window. Without a word they stayed like that for a while.

"Everything was against us - she was only on the island for a year; her parents thought we were miles apart socially, the village people thought I was too big for my boots and then -" His voice became strangled, limiting his own words, and Eilidh wondered if she would say, 'I know about that night. I know.'

But she didn't, and John said nothing about the

accident. Instead he looked into Eilidh's face and saw all of it: intelligent eyes which absorbed all her compassion, still mouth intending only to listen.

"And then, Eilidh - Helen - left the island and I never saw her again. I didn't know about...you know, a baby. It was wrong, what we did, but it was Eilidh who suffered, not me. It must have been terrible for her. If only I'd known!" Eilidh saw that his hands had balled up into fists, his head bowed again, shut in on himself and the past. "But I didn't know," he said at last. "I had no idea where they went to live. I knew nothing, not one pinprick about her family's whereabouts, and I began to believe she never really cared. At least, I told myself that. It was my treaty with reality, Eilidh. It was the only way I could cope."

"I think I can understand that," Eilidh said hesitantly, "and... I think I know now why you've been more distant with me. I remind you of my grandmother. And I guess you're totally wiped out when you remember...is - is that it?"

He couldn't answer her. Words were tangling up in his throat, she knew that. But he nodded, and she made herself somehow take the long, long four steps towards him. Then, with an instinctive, unthinking movement, she knelt down next to his chair, and put her head on his arm. A silence developed between them, until she felt his other arm encircling her.

"I can't help feeling, now that I've got my daughter's family with me," John said, and his voice had a cracked sound, "that God has given me a second chance of happiness," He turned Eilidh around slightly to face him and he asked her the one question now on his mind.

"What was she like? Your mum - my daughter - what was she like?"

Eilidh tried to think objectively. It was hard to describe her mother. You didn't always look carefully at the people you love, and live with. They were just there.

"Eilidh?"

She nodded, as though choosing the words to describe her mother, and then looked up into her grandfather's eyes. "Well, she wasn't beautiful exactly, maybe pretty would describe her better. She had a lovely smile, and this trick of opening her eyes wide when she was listening to you...and she looked too young to be my mum, everybody said so! She had bags of style, too, even if we were stony broke most of the time.

Some Saturdays she'd drag us over to the posh suburbs for their jumble sales, and that's where she got all her clothes. Talk about wearing your clothes with flair! That way, she could be bohemian one day, a career girl the next, and plain mumsy when no one was looking!"

"She sounded a lot of fun," John prodded her gently.

"Oh, she was! She used to sing a lot, everything from nursery rhymes to soppy Country & Western, but that all stopped when my father took off - my excuse for a father, that is - and we never heard her singing after that."

Suddenly, this was the last subject Eilidh wanted to be talking about, and she said, almost sharply, "There's something I wanted to ask you - "

"Sure," John interrupted, "but first, have you a photo of your mum?" There was something non-negotiable about the request.

"Yes, I put all our photos into the bureau. I'll get them." Getting up, she crossed over to the bureau, and opened it. By concentrating on the mechanism of finding the photograph, she managed to blank out her mind, preventing an ambush of memories.

"That's the best one, I think," she said, handing John the photograph. While the man stared down at the daughter he had never seen, would never see, Eilidh continued to stare into space as if it were an activity. She couldn't bring herself to look.

She didn't have to. It was all imprinted in her memory, the lop-sided photograph of her mother, eyes huge and smiling, dark hair cascading freely over one shoulder, exuding an assurance of perfect health. It had been taken one year ago, on a summer's day.

Carefully, tenderly, John Paterson handled the photograph, saying, "May I keep this for a little while? I can have a copy made, get a good frame, put it - " He stopped in mid-sentence, his face twisting into a mask of grief and pain. "If only I'd known, if only!"

Eilidh stood still, listening to the drumroll cadence of the words. She grieved for the loss of what he never had, but she could not console him. There was no consolation. Instead she changed the subject, saying softly, "Can I ask you now?"

Lifting his eyes from the snapshot of his daughter, he said, "Go on, then, ask."

"Are you sad, John? Are you sad about your Eilidh, and how things took a wrong turning for you both?" She looked directly at him, from close. He looked right back, and his eyes smiled, dark and distant, as if moving back in time. As if he knew things she didn't.

"Sad? No, Eilidh. What if I'd never known her? That would have been sad."

CHAPTER 10

Over the next week, Eilidh arranged and re-arranged the photographic display in the mirror-backed alcove. She felt tempted to display John's soldier snapshot right beside Paul's school photo, but hesitated. John had told Paul the truth, but until everybody knew, Eilidh felt she shouldn't jump the gun with any revelations. John - grandfather - would have to do the 'telling', not her, and not Paul.

It was Paul who now broke into her thoughts. He uncurled himself from behind the dining-room table with some difficulty and dumped several screwed-up sheets of paper into the bin. "That's how far I got on with the History Assignment!" He drilled the History book a hateful look, but picked it up and said, "I'm off to Anna's. We'll both do better if we conquer History together."

"Ugh! Call the doctor! I'm coming down with an infectious disease - or is it that crawlers make me sick?" Eilidh joked, taking a backward pace to survey her home-making efforts.

"Do I detect a little negativity here, sis?" Holding a half-smile in place, he scraped back the chair noisily. "Jealous because Anna's once, twice, three times a beauty?"

"Don't be daft! It's not just sour grapes on my part
...just because you've got Anna and I've got no - " She
slid into the seat her brother had vacated and fiddled with
the pens on the table. "No, I'm just all strung out at the
thought of starting this assignment." From teasing-and-
sarcasm to a light despair. "I'm way behind the others,
and I've only got this afternoon to do it. And John's
collecting seedlings from the ferry...Paul, you couldn't
take Ellis with you, could you? "

"Nice try, sis. No chance!"

"You're sure about that?"

"You want it in writing? - Bye!" And he was off, with
that loose, easy walk of his, exuding confidence with
every step.

Eilidh gave his retreating back a something-less-than
friendly look, calling after him, "If you ask me, the male
sex is still getting the best of this equality deal!" She
didn't look forward to being cooped up with her little
sister when she was going full throttle. Ellis, plus the
assignment, was guaranteed to drive anyone to the brink
of insanity. Eilidh stared at the white emptiness of the
notepad and then hurled herself into World War II. She
wrote angrily, digging the pencil savagely into the lined
page.

Her favourite programme over, Ellis stomped into the
kitchen and plumped herself down beside her big sister.
The little voice piped, subtle as a sledgehammer, "Can
I want - can I have a biscuit, and juice...and can I go out
to play with the doggie?"

"Mmmph? What doggie? Later. Let me write this,
will you?"

"I want choc-it biscuit!" Ellis formed her little hands into iron balls, ready to do a spot of drumming on the table.

Eilidh dropped the desperately-maintained smile. "Look, no more biscuits. I'll make you toast later - okay?"

"Don't want toast!" Ellis protested. "The cracking noise gives me sore ears!" And she began drumming her heels against the chair leg to prove how strongly she felt about it.

Through clenched teeth, Eilidh muttered, "Oh, for Pete's sake, how DO you reach a three-year old in an appeal to reason?"

But Ellis was like a needle that got stuck in the groove of a record, and all that came out was 'juice, biscuit, doggie'. Her voice gathered momentum and Eilidh was perfectly aware that nothing short of a bulldozer crashing through the wall would stop her sister now. All by herself, Ellis could make more noise than debating politicians in the House of Commons. The stories began marching out mercilessly...the time she losted her kitten, the dead rabbit on the road with its meat hanging out, how Paul made a bad face at her when she was chewing the gum she found on the pavement....

"Oh, go away and play!" Eilidh interrupted crossly, and got up to give her a chocolate biscuit. 'Peace at any price' she admitted, gathering up more papers with furious energy. Ellis wriggled down from her chair and ran full tilt through the door. "Don't go out of the gate!" Eilidh called after her, deciding, not for the first time, that her younger sister had been born with the compulsion to crash through life.

However, the quiet emptiness Ellis left behind didn't help the creation of the assignment, and what she had written so far had merely made the obvious unintelligible. She chewed her pencil, her head filled with thoughts about the Bible readings they listened to as a family. Listened to daily, but not always heard. But now, as the hands of the large kitchen clock jumped past the minutes, Eilidh's mind swirled in a miasma of questions.

Was God's love really the sloppy and sentimental kind of love she had associated with him in the past? No, from their readings it was obvious that he was more than...than some divine Santa Claus. Or, as she had thought in the last few months, an absentee landlord with his phone off the hook? It seemed to be much, much more than that. A love that seeks out my highest good? she asked herself, half-amused at the recall of churchy jargon. She stared out of the window, not focusing on anything in particular. If that was so, what did it mean for her, now?

"Huh - all this won't get my assignment done!" she said aloud, and went into the kitchen to switch on the kettle. These criss-crossing, confusing thoughts came rarely, but when they did they unsettled her with their appeal to the emotion. She knew she was struggling with a fear of being helpless - a fear of giving up her self government and completely re-surrendering to another. This Jesus. But still she struggled. After all, when God was running her life, everything had gone wrong, hadn't it? "I've come through a lot recently and managed okay. So, I can manage my own life, can't I?"

She rubbed her forehead sheepishly. Chasing poor Ellis away, and still no assignment! "Ellis!" she shouted through the open window. "Juice! C'mon - " Making a clicking sound with her tongue, she went outside. "Ellis? You playing hide and seek? Okay, I'll count - one, two, miss a few, ninety-nine, a hundred. Ready or not, here I come!"

The air was dry and warm, full of sunlight; but as Eilidh searched the garden, the garage, the greenhouse, she began to feel a chill of isolation. Where on earth was Ellis?

Her mind raced, seeking possible hiding places. She sat down on the garden bench, then stood up again, her nerves on edge. She pushed back the panic that was creeping over her. "Ellis!" she called over and over again, her voice unnaturally loud. No answering sound broke the stillness. She walked under the branches of trees surrounding the house. They, too, seemed to wait, listening in the silence. In the brightness, in the solemn daylight, Eilidh suddenly felt very alone.

Mentally pulling herself together, she hurried back into the house and dialled Anna's phone number. Anna's voice came over the wire immediately. Hurriedly, she informed Eilidh that they were all on their way out to town - including Paul - and they'd buy blow-bubbles and plasticine for Ellis. "...so she won't feel she's missing out."

'In other words, she ain't there,' Eilidh thought as she said cheerio and dialled again, this time the Macpherson's house. Please, please say you've seen her, she begged silently into the mouthpiece.

Mrs Macpherson's voice was warm and friendly. "Oh, Eilidh, Ronnie will be so pleased you phoned. If only he was in! But he's away down to the beach with the dog.... Have I seen Ellis? No. She's probably at the Murray's - you're not worried about her, are you dear?"

"Oh no, Mrs Macpherson - s'okay...she'll be in the garden somewhere," Eilidh lied, her panic mounting. How could she say, 'Of course I'm worried. Ellis is gone - checked out - history - flipped. I'm worried crazy!' Instead she said bye, hung up the phone, and leaned against the wall, staring down at the deep-pile carpet as if she had nothing better to do. Slowly she slipped down until she was sitting on the floor. Where could Ellis be? Not at the neighbours anyway, and John was at the ferry - so where else? She allowed her mind to rove outside the garden gate. Miles and miles of beach, rocks - the sea. The sea!

Eilidh got up and ran out of the house, down the path, over the road and across to the beach. She didn't notice how the sky shone deep blue, and how the white clouds, fat and lazy, drifted across it. She only noticed that for miles the lonely beach wandered with just a few seagulls for company. No sign of Ellis.

She ran on, away from the sand, up towards Creag Dubh (Black Rock), a steep cliff overlooking part of the sea. Each step towards the cliff was punctuated with a word. "Oh! God! Find! Ellis!" Over and over again, until she found herself saying instead, "Oh God, find Eilidh."

CHAPTER 11

When she reached the edge of the cliff, Eilidh stood for a moment, gazing down into the endless stretch of inky sea. The water gurgled and lifted its heavy burden of sea-weed, up and down, up and down, as it rose and fell with the waves. There wasn't a beach down there, only the cold, forbidding, bottomless ocean. Again she shivered despite the warmth of the day.

She looked up into the white-flecked sky, angry. "I have a right to be angry," she told God. "Why don't you come down off that throne and help ME? Why did you let Ellis run off? Why did you leave me in charge of Ellis - my mum should be looking after her, not me! And why did you take mum? Why?"

The sunlight winked across the sea, and she hated its brightness. She wanted only to think about Ellis - not about her mother. And she didn't know how to stop the feeling of nothingness, the emptiness that would never be filled.

And just for a moment, she allowed herself to remember. How different things used to be...her mother laughing, tossing Ellis like a rag doll, the little girl's helpless laughter - but that was centuries ago, all gone, long gone. And Eilidh wished she hadn't opened up the wound running from the present to the past.

"No," she said. "No." Moving again, she made her feet start walking back down towards the beach. "No, I can't blame Mum, or God. It's no one's fault but mine, I wanted to get rid of Ellis...it's all my fault!"

Following that admission, every bad thing she had ever done, no matter how insignificant, paraded through her head. She ran on, her heart thumping, thumping, thumping; louder, louder, louder.

Finally, she could run no more, and she collapsed onto the beach, her arms tightly wrapped around herself, her eyes squeezed shut against the glare.

And then, she heard the high-pitched voice. "Eilidh! Eil-idh!" Unmistakable. Ellis came careering from behind a rock, a large, wet dog in tow. At the other end of a lead was Ronnie.

"Hi, Eilidh," Ronnie grinned. "She can't half talk, this sister of yours! Who winds her up every morning? Anyway, hope you appreciate this spot of baby-sitting."

"Appreciate?" she echoed. She was on her feet suddenly, angry, so angry, she couldn't contain it all in her body. "Appreciate! HOW DARE YOU!" She stopped right beside him, waving her forefinger under his nose, anger disfiguring her face. In the background Ellis - as if to forestall a row - chanted "It's not me fault...it's not me fault - "

"That's coming on a bit strong, isn't it?" Ronnie interrupted, his brown eyes uncertain. "What's got you jumping down my throat, anyway?" Eilidh's anger drove his smile away, and he pulled his body further away from hers. "She didn't mean that quite the way it sounded," he muttered to Ellis, who was by now only interested in throwing sand over the dog.

"Ronnie Macpherson, I meant every word!"

"Are you sure you don't have a more murderous look than that, Eilidh?" he said, peering down into her face. "Just stood up in your pram and chucked out your rattle, right?"

"Very funny. Okay...thanks very much for looking after her. That was sweet of you. If you ever, EVER, do that again without telling me...I'll - I'll have your eye-brows shaved off!"

He covered the offending articles quickly, and there was the sound of his smothered laughter. "How can you stand there and be so cool about it?" Eilidh shouted, her head almost exploding with pent-up anger. She couldn't believe what she had just gone through, and Ronnie could only react by trying hard not to laugh.

"Look, you're freaked enough to cover the situation for both of us, and have some leftover!" His smile faded as he folded his arms across his chest. "Look, Eilidh...I was innocently going for a walk with Lassie here...and your sister appeared from nowhere. She said she had told you she was going to play with doggie. Honestly, it was only a bit of humanitarian effort on my part!"

"Then, you failed. You failed miserably." She shot out more hedgehog prickles of sarcasm to protect herself from weakening.

"I'm just trying to be friendly...and you're not making it very easy."

"Huh! As if that has anything to do with anything." Unable to stand another second under his now puzzled eyes, she turned away. But he pressed down hard on her shoulders, almost thumping her into a sitting position on the sand. Then, flopping down beside her, he got back to the argument.

"Well, Eilidh, excuse me for living! What is this anyway - killing the bearer of news, like in the Bible, or Ancient Greece, or somewhere? You should be over the moon that Ellis is okay! Shouldn't you? Instead of behaving like some headless hen!"

At this, Eilidh turned to her sister, drawing her near, and planted a kiss on the tiny round blob of a nose. The little girl, oblivious to all the fuss, watched as her bare toes squished through the wet sand.

Ronnie still had that look on his face. The look that said go on...put your head on straight and explain. "I'm being quiet now," he said, "so that means it's your turn to talk."

Eilidh remained silent. Ronnie cocked his head at her, saying, "Let's talk."

"What d'you think we're doing," she replied with an exaggerated expression of humour. "I saw your lips move, didn't I?"

"I mean really talk."

"How d'you think I feel?" she sat ramrod straight, facing him. "My stomach's got...you know, butterflies, moths, small birds...." She tried hard to be funny but her voice shook. She gulped some air and struggled to control the quake in her voice. "I thought I had lost her...I looked everywhere, but she had just vanished into thin air...and I was to blame! And then, I was so angry that Mum had died and - ."

"And left you with too much responsibility. Is that it?" His voice was soft and quiet, full of hidden strength. "Poor Eilidh. You've been dragged into adulthood and responsibility. And you don't want it. You want to be young and carefree. You want to be the little girl again - wee, dependent. Don't you?"

She could not answer. Her mouth was full of the need to cry. She knew she was giving in to some babyish weakness, wanting to tell. Wanting to be comforted. Ronnie saw it all and his concern made him clumsy. Reaching out, he tried to take her hand, but she yanked it away. A large fist inside her throat was squeezing, until the tears spilled over and streamed down her face.

All at once the pain was too much to take and she covered her face with both hands and began to sob. 'Oh, Mum, Mum...why did you die and leave us? she demanded silently. How could you do this to us? How could you leave me with this hurt? I - can't - bear - it!'

Eilidh felt Ronnie put his arms carefully around her shoulders, and hold her, just as if she was something very precious that he didn't want to break. Meanwhile wave after wave of anguish and grief racked her body, making her gasp for air, unable to control her crying.

"It's okay, it's okay. You need to cry," Ronnie whispered. It wasn't good for you to bottle it up. You need to mourn your mum." She leaned against his chest while he spoke and then for a long time afterwards while the tears dried up.

They sat on, letting the afternoon flow over them, and watched the screaming, wheeling Ellis disturb all the guillemots and herring gulls. Eilidh just wanted to sit there, and absorb Ronnie's strength. The day was lasting forever and she wanted to release all the emotions tangling up inside her - sorrow, fear, loneliness, bitterness, and love. And she wanted to remember.

Staring out across the endless sea, she was amazed at how her mind had noticed and registered so many details of her mother's last few days. While Eilidh had been mindlessly going through the motions, just getting through the hours and minutes and seconds, her brain had been storing up pictures. Reaching the hospital in the ambulance and being totally unaware of the journey from home; a desperate, fervent wish to be a smoker - anything to pass the time in that horrible waiting room; gobbling up Mars Bars from the vending machine without even tasting them, and the resulting sickish feeling; not knowing what to do with hands and legs while the doctor spoke to her. And then, sitting down carefully on the ugly tubular chair as if her body would fall apart if she moved suddenly.

The time sequence of the memory slipped a cog, and there were more of the kaleidoscope of images. They circled, and the unspoken word 'orphans' hung in the disinfected air. Afterwards, there were all the repetitive 'sorry's' whispered under the cold glare of fluorescent lighting. Was there nothing else people could say? What could they say? What words could people find to say in the grief and terror of the day?

And then - Eilidh made designs in the sand with one finger - the poor pretence of functioning, sleepwalking at the funeral, and after that, the hollow, lost feeling. "I tried so hard not to think about Mum," she said aloud, shifting restlessly. "It wouldn't do me any good, that's what I thought. I'd fall to pieces. Or it would make me so mad...."

Hearing herself, she didn't think she'd made much sense, but Ronnie was following her mind. "Mad against God, is that what you mean?" He had caught on and finished the idea before she had really thought it to herself.

She managed a watery smile, and nodded in agreement. "That's it. Only, I didn't know properly, till today," - absently, she sifted sand through her fingers - "that it was God I was bitter against. It's been so weird. See, even now when I feel I have everything - security, new friends, plenty of money - suddenly, out of the blue, I'm just...overwhelmed with sadness." She stopped speaking then. She was staring hard at her hand spread out over the sand. Then she looked straight into Ronnie's face and she felt her mouth trying to find out how to continue.

"After our Bible reading the other night, some words stuck in my mind. Something about being clothed with joy, not wearing sackcloth. And... have I been determined to hang onto my sackcloth!"

They were suddenly sprinkled with wet as the vintage dog bounded up beside them and began to shake himself vigorously. Ronnie took no notice, his eyes still feeding on Eilidh, and she could have hugged him, because he knew her need to unload everything. He knew it, and she felt a great rush of warmth towards him for staying still.

"See, a long time ago - well, it seems a long time ago - I asked Jesus into my life. Then...when Mum became ill...and died...I blamed God. Not quite the intelligent approach, I know!" Her mouth twisted into the travesty of a smile. "I guess none of us have the monopoly on that, huh? Anyway, as far as God was concerned, my brain was definitely out-to-lunch. But I've never, never, felt right since then. I tried to ignore it - ."

Again, Ronnie finished the sentence for her. "But you couldn't."

For a silent moment they watched Ellis splashing at some pool water with her chubby little hands, her eyes laughing. "No," Eilidh finally said. "Instead I felt empty. If my life wasn't the Lord's, then - why was I here? What was the meaning of my life? What was the meaning of my mum's life? Was it a waste? Surely it wasn't a waste!" Eilidh burned with a kind of fire as she spoke.

"Did your mum - did she believe?" Ronnie asked.

"Yes. Just weeks before she died, she told us she gave her life to Jesus. She said she felt enfolded in Jesus as she lay there in that bed."

"Then," Ronnie said, studying her face, "her life wasn't a waste." After those out-of-time moments they fell silent, and simply watched the lines of waves breaking on the shore, the black-headed gulls flying in a line over the surface of the water, the noisy interplay between dog and child. Eilidh's head danced with the light and colour and laughter of it all, and felt a crazy joy. It wasn't a waste!

"Eilidh," Ronnie began to speak. His general posture was, by now, on the slow side of laid back, he appeared relaxed to the point of dozing off...and yet his voice was tense. "Eilidh, can I tell you what's going on in my head? Your mum had peace with God, didn't she? And now, well, there's life after life and she's now in heaven. It was a shortish life, but full of meaning. But when you think of all the lost folk in this world...what life does to people.

I mean, look at my father. Bitter, oh boy, is he bitter!"

Eilidh could hear him swallowing and clearing his throat rustily before he went on. "Even as a boy, my father was everything that I didn't want to be when I grew up. Isn't that some statement, huh? He's probably, deep down, as good as the next guy, but hate for John Paterson has become as much part of him as the red cells in his bloodstream. Believe me, there's no higher prison walls than those a mind builds up with that kind of hatred!" He took a deep, steadying breath and black humour entered his voice. "Eilidh, in my loving, happy home, the first lesson I learned was to keep my mouth shut about certain things. So, after years of living in that set-up, I needed something, well, different."

He stopped speaking for a moment, then he spoke quickly, as if he wanted to get it all out. "When I went to college last year, I started learning things to help me make a living. But all the time, what I was really wanting to know, wanting to be told was - how do I live?"

"And did you - find out, I mean?"

He screwed up his eyes against the sun. Then, lifting his eyes back to Eilidh, he smiled and nodded.

"You...too?" she asked.

"Yes, Eilidh. Hard to believe, huh? Especially after reacting to your brother's fists in the way I did! I'm telling you, if there were points on some Christian scale of nought to ten, then I definitely score lowish."

At his words, Eilidh felt - rising up inside her - feelings so strong she didn't know she could voice them. In her thoughts she tiptoed around the words, but when she finally spoke her voice was firm. "And I'd score zero."

"Hang on a minute, I said 'if there WERE'. Eilidh, look at me!" Knowing the way her thoughts were running, he moved closer and pressed her arm. "There isn't such a thing as a Christian scale of nought to ten, is there? Okay, so you failed, and okay so I failed. Badly. But there's forgiveness, right? And even if we did become everything we dreamed of...."

"Go on."

"God wouldn't love me, love you, any more than he loves us right this minute. Would he?"

"No, I guess not," Eilidh's face split into a sudden smile. "Wow! That's some thought, isn't it?" Silent now, they watched Ellis laboriously digging a hole to Australia.

"Hey, c'mon!" Suddenly grabbing her hand, Ronnie pulled Eilidh to her feet. "Let's shut our mouths, open our eyes and ears...and we'll recapture your lost youth, Eilidh! Let's have some fun!"

"Fun? Oh-oh...I think I've just had my first flash of women's intuition - what does he mean by fun?" Eilidh hoped her voice reflected careless teasing rather than the missed beat of her heart. With her falling-down hair and sticky face she knew she looked like the wreck of the Hesperus.

Ronnie groaned, his face folding into a lazy amused grin. "How does that saying go again? He who dares, wins; he who hesitates - don't! No, there's nothing tricky going on in my mind. No hidden agenda - I promise you!" He scooped a huge handful of sand and aimed it at her, demonstrating 'fun'.

"Okay, whatever you say, Professor," she grinned widely, warming to the exercise. Hand in hand they began skipping up and down the beach, bobbing and weaving out of the water, circling around Ellis and the dog. Then, out of breath, they stopped to play noughts and crosses in the sand.

A wave rolled in and washed over Eilidh's 'O'. They stood close together now, watching the wave pull back, leaving behind only a puddled trace of her mark. Without looking at Ronnie, Eilidh spoke. Her voice was soft, low and slow. "Ronnie, d'you mind if I ask you something? - I'm going to ask it anyway!"

"What's that?"

"Don't you wish we were different kinds of people? I mean, not being hostages to the past, and all that blah."

"I know what you mean. There's no second-hand hostility on my part. But you know that, don't you?" At his next words, the sunlight danced for Eildih, and her head felt disconnected. "Eilidh, do you like me?"

"Yes."

"How much?"

"Very, very much." And then, the question burst out from her as though she couldn't contain it. "Ronnie - d'you think of me as just a kid?"

She turned round to catch the quick fleeting look he gave her and the words, "No, I don't. I wish I did."

CHAPTER 12

After the Bible-reading that night, Eilidh tucked her sleeping sister under the Paddington Bear quilt. It was a family joke that Ellis called the worship 'tired time', and would grab both pyjamas and Bible when John rounded them all up. Now, as Eilidh stared down at the peaceful face she whispered another 'thank you.' She bent down and dropped a big, sloppy kiss on her forehead.

"If you're looking for me, I'm watching a video upstairs," Paul called from the doorway.

"Wot - no Anna?"

"No." Paul's best feature wasn't his control, and now he wrinkled his face like a prune.

Eilidh tucked an imaginary violin beneath her chin and played a lament. Paul shot her a venomous glance, so she stopped, saying quickly, "Okay, okay. How desperate are things?"

"Above-average desperate." He picked up a discarded rag doll and squeezed it with great intensity, then flung it back onto the floor. "In town today, I left Anna in the cafe while I ran round the shops. When I came back, well - it was like the first day of Harrods sale. Queues around the block. Of admiring guys, that is! One in particular was trying to muscle in on her." Eilidh recognized the non-verbal signals, the flashing eye, as he continued. "And, would you believe it - she fell for it! He's taking her to some disco. He's a real smoothie too. Wouldn't I like to tie him to a rocket and launch him into outer - "

"Wow," Eilidh said, knowing she had to say something, but not quite knowing the right thing to say. She didn't know how to lessen his humiliation.

"Aw, why am I telling you all this?"

"I don't know."

"What do I do?"

"Well, you could always become a monk," Eilidh grinned. "Or what about a re-run of Gunfight at the O.K. Corral - you know, like you had with Ronnie?"

"I should know better" - he said with a contemptuous toss of the head - "than to discuss important things with you. Forget it. Over and out!"

"Look," Eilidh said, folding away Ellis's jogging suit, "don't be so wet! You can overdo caring, you know. Those last few days, Anna's had as much freedom as if she was in prison. If it's not you overpowering her, it's her smother-mother. Bet she almost feels as if she's wearing a collar!"

Eilidh saw her brother's eyes looking at her with something she had to name confusion. "Is any of this getting through to you, Paul?" she asked, as she navigated past a doll's house and scattered building blocks.

With an air of hugely controlled patience he said, "I've got to hand it to you females! So now I've got to get devious and start using my brain - don't be around too much, don't hang out your feelings too much, don't - "

"Oh, Paul, you're making it all sound so complicated!"

Eilidh said, and her face collapsed into laughter. "You have got a bad dose of the glums, haven't you?"

"Huh, s'okay for you! Strolling through life without any worries. What would you know anyway?" He fixed her with a withering stare before charging up the stairs.

Despite her teasing words, Eilidh understood how her brother felt. She didn't want things to change either. She wanted this summer to go on forever, with things just as they were now. And yet, things were changing....

"Eilidh - coffee?" John's voice, calling from the kitchen, cut across any further meditation.

The aroma of freshly-brewed coffee hung in the air, and plaintive fiddle music from the radio washed around the kitchen. For a while, Eilidh sat there at the table and let the peace of the evening surround her. John was staring out of the window watching the sun disappearing behind the horizon in a soft glow, turning the whole sky and sea into a painter's palette. Without turning round he said, "Eilidh, there was a phone call for you, when you were putting Ellis to bed." And then, "It was Ronnie Macpherson."

"Oh!" She had caught something odd in his voice, a nuance that unsettled her, but still she went to the extension gladly. She was impatiently listening to the ringing tone when a hand closed over her own. It was John.

"What - "

"Please. Don't."

"Oops, sorry! Were you wanting to use the phone?"

"No, not really. Look Eilidh, I...I'd rather you didn't phone Ronnie." His eyes, looking into hers, seemed to issue a plea. "I'd rather you didn't get involved with him."

"But - why?" Eilidh asked, her voice betraying surprise. She laid the phone gently on its rest, and let her hand lie there for a moment, as if carved from stone.

"I've nothing against Ronnie but...it wouldn't be an easy friendship. Don't ask me to explain right now, but I...I don't want to see you hurt. That's all."

Eilidh sat down again to her coffee and cake. She was quiet, merely going through the motions of eating. She wasn't tasting anything, only following one mechanical mouthful with another. John sat down opposite her at the pine table, making something of a ritual in sweetening his coffee. She didn't look up, but she could feel the circles of sadness he was bogged down in, and she didn't like feeling it; above all she didn't like him feeling it. She sat somewhere between sad and bewildered. Why did the past have to affect her, anyway?

"Ronnie's father doesn't need to know," she said finally. She bit into her cake to give her time to think of a more persuasive argument. Chewing and swallowing didn't activate her brain any further, so she repeated, "He doesn't need to know any - "

"Listen," he cut her off, leaning slightly towards her. "It's not only that. I understand how you might feel, Eilidh. You know, I was your age once."

At that, she stopped his talk. Stopped the listening. "How dare you," she said quietly. "Just because you and my grandmother...made a mistake." Standing up, she could feel her palms moist as she held onto the back of the chair, but, still, she was aware of a sense of power. Power, total and merciless over another human being. In that moment, she used it. Her tone was icy now as she said,

"Credit me with more sense that that, huh?" She turned and walked away.

His voice stopped her progress to the door.

"Eilidh." She waited, one hand reaching for the door handle.

"There's nothing you can say, is there?" she said, and her voice was lightly contemptuous. Not looking back, she left the room.

She didn't remember stumbling out of the house into the garden, but there she was, walking into the dying light of a summer's day; and wishing there was some way of getting through the rest of her life without having to live it. With my big mouth and my desire to self-destruct, living isn't going to be easy, she thought wryly. "Lord, help."

Walking through the garden on rubbery legs, she paused only to pick up some soiled flower petals that lay in drifts beside the bare-stemmed flower. The work of Ellis, she thought grimly. What a disaster we've all been for that poor man!

Needing more time to think, to pull it all together, she walked round and round mindlessly, head down. But it made no difference how far she walked, how much she stared down at her marching feet, she just kept on seeing her grandfather's face.

She knew what she saw in his eyes. A plea. 'Please don't.' As a granddaughter she was supposed to need his help, not the other way around. But she knew what she saw. The look had lasted only a moment but the hurt behind it had coloured his whole life, like ink dropped in clear water.

He didn't know that SHE knew, and she felt poisoned by her knowledge. Should she say something? Was she entitled to say something?

"I can't let him down now, whatever happens," she said aloud, her mind suddenly focusing. "Go and talk to him," she then drilled herself as she advanced towards the house, "and this time get it right!" Stepping resolutely into the thickly-carpeted hallway, she contemplated Ronnie with a minute quantum of confusion. "Lord, make him understand. You're in charge."

John Paterson was still sitting at the table, his mug of coffee untouched. Looking up, he met her gaze and they both spoke at the same time.

"Sorry!"

"I'm sorry."

They both smiled, but John's smile was tired, as if he'd worn it too long, so Eilidh added quickly, "just write it off as growing pains on my part, will you?"

"And what will my excuse be then?" he asked, almost teasing. He gestured for her to sit down and she began to speak with a sheepish little smile.

"You must be fed up to the back teeth with us, especially of me!"

Smiling at how bluntly Eilidh put it, he shook his head as they slid back into normal domestic bliss, drinking lukewarm coffee and trying to think of what to say next.

Eilidh spoke first. "I won't see Ronnie again."

"And is that bearable?"

"Oh, I'll live." She felt uncomfortable under the constancy of his gaze and wriggled in the chair.

"Eilidh?" he said. "Someday I'll explain."

She pushed about the crumbs on her plate, her eyes lowered, every inch a hypocrite. Should she keep quiet, pretend she knew nothing? On an impulse she looked up, saying hurriedly, "Seanair - can I call you 'Seanair'? That's what Anna calls her grandfather." He nodded and she went on, studying him sadly. "I couldn't...couldn't stand to be one more of the things that's working to hurt you. I couldn't be that. I don't want to be that. So I'll keep away from Ronnie, if that's what you really want. But," her voice slipped through the shadowy kitchen, "but see, I know about the past. The accident, and all that."

She swallowed, unable to speak for a moment. She pleated the cotton place mat between her fingers and then smoothed it out on the table. "I only want to say that...whatever has happened in your past, there's forgiveness in Jesus."

He looked up sharply, and then looked down again. His lips started to form a word, but he didn't speak. Instead he scraped back his chair and crossed over to the window. It was hard trying to talk to him without being able to see his face, and yet she felt a little smile lifting the corners of her mouth. "There! I've managed to say the name of Jesus. If only you knew how, tonight, I planned and schemed ways of telling you...."

"Telling me what?" He turned around to face her.

"That I've come back. To Jesus. You see, Seanair, every night you read the worship...it felt as if Jesus was there, just reminding me about himself."

She spoke quietly. She was having to go slowly, feel her way with words. The halting voice was digging deep, and she sat there, as if staring inside herself, and she was amazed at what she was learning.

In those stretched seconds, the tick of the kitchen clock sounded solemn and loud. Her grandfather sat down once again and shifted uneasily in his chair as Eilidh went on. "Seanair, once we're forgiven, Jesus comes to live in us and change our lives. We can't change ourselves. He does the changing."

"And what if you can't forgive yourself? What then?"

The words surprised her with their harshness, and he must have realised it because he took a minute before he continued, softly, very softly, "what if...when you think of God...all you can see is the dead, dead face of a little boy - and no amount of forgiveness is going to bring him back?   And there's just nowhere that you can buy a silencer for the conscience on the market. Is there?"

From Paul's room came the muffled wailing of some rock group, but Eilidh, who had listened to her grandfather's words, now listened only to his silence. His face was bleak, unguarded, vulnerable. Suddenly determined to reopen old wounds, he said, "Eilidh, for years after, I could hardly look in a mirror. I avoided my own reflection like a deadly enemy - do you know that?"

"I don't know, Seanair." Eilidh answered him. "I can only imagine."

"No one can imagine someone else's pain, Eilidh," he said. "You can't imagine how I felt at that time, any more than I could imagine how that little boy's parents felt. That's how I can't forgive myself. Because of their pain."

She took a deep breath and said aloud, "So you're willing, then, to lose heaven just because you can't forgive yourself? What a price to pay! Oh John - Seanair

- just say to God 'Here...here's a failed life, Lord. Work on it!'"

He started to shake his head 'no' but stopped in the middle as they both heard Mrs Murray's loud "Cooeee!" and "Anybody in?" And it was all left unsaid.

For a while, the neighbours exchanged polite pleasantries until, eventually, Mrs Murray sat down and came to the point of her visit. "I'm trying to organise lifts for the parents evening in school next week. I didn't think you'd be going, John, seeing you're only their guardian, but as I said to my husband, well, there's no harm in asking."

John listened patiently to her prattle, while the beginning of a smile hovered in one corner of his mouth. When Mrs Murray's monologue had come to a halt, he took a sip of coffee and said, "I'm going."

"Oh! Oh, that's fine!" Mrs Murray, disguising her surprise, accepted Eilidh's offer of a cup of coffee. She made a few polite, twittery noises until Eilidh saw her lean forward and clear her throat, the way she did when she was curious and her curiosity was unfed and unquieted. "Aren't you the lucky one, Eilidh, to have found such a good home!"

Knowing Mrs Murray's ability to take every breath down in shorthand, and use it to fuel local gossip, Eilidh was totally unprepared for John's next statement.

"Oh no, I'm the lucky one. Lucky...." He paused a moment or two. It seemed to Eilidh that he didn't want to say any more. But he did.

"I'm lucky to have such a granddaughter."

CHAPTER 13

A week later, and John Paterson's revelation was still the talk of the community. It was the main topic of conversation in Eilidh's class at school, outshining even the turbulent topic of Paul and Anna's on-off romance. It was whispered with subdued excitement by John's ever-increasing number of customers, hoping to gain some hot news along with their bedding plants. It was even noted with compassion and understanding at the local church which John Paterson and his new family had started to attend.

During that time Eilidh wondered if Ronnie, too, knew that she was John Paterson's granddaughter. And if so, how did he feel about it? She didn't have long to mull over the possibilities for one afternoon Ronnie, astride a magnificent motorbike, came roaring up to 'Fasgadh' just as Eilidh was hanging out the washing.

"Oh, no!" she whispered, fighting with clothes pegs and billowing sheets. "Please go away!" Pretending she didn't see him, she stared upwards over the tops of the trees, where a procession of high-minded clouds raced, gilded by sunshine.

"Hi there!"

No miracle had happened. There he was, striding

towards her, helmet in hand. He smiled his warm, sudden smile and a star shot across her mind. Already her imagination was doing cartwheels as she pictured herself jumping behind Ronnie on the motorbike, then roaring away into the sunset, with John Paterson and Roderick Macpherson following on - .

"Are you hanging the sheets on yourself, or the washing line?" Ronnie laughed, unravelling a snowy-white sheet which seemed to have draped itself around her. "How about going for a ride on my cousin's bike? Beauty, isn't it?"

"Yes! No! I mean, the bike - is a beauty. But no, I can't go for a ride..." she trailed off, looking around to see if John Paterson was observing this situation comedy from one of the windows.

"S'okay, I've got a helmet for you. And the nearest place to break the speed limit is hundreds of miles away, on the mainland. So you'll be safe enough." She was suddenly very aware of the way he could smile with half his mouth, but only for a second, for John Paterson had materialized from nowhere and was bearing down on them like a middle-aged dynamo.

"Yes? Can I help you?" he asked.

Not surprisingly, there was silence. At last, Ronnie put in his request, very politely. Eilidh studied her grand-father's face, but she couldn't tell anything from his expression. Twisting her fingers together nervously, she waited for the rebuff.

It didn't come. John Paterson merely said, "All right, Ronnie, I'll let Eilidh go with you just this once. But I think she's got a few things to tell you. Yes?"

Nodding in agreement, Eilidh said as casually as she could, "I'll just change into my jeans, then. Won't be long."

Showing a tortoise-like lethargy, she tried not to break into a run as soon as she was out of their sight. Once inside the house, however, she bounded up the stairs, followed by Ellis, who could always be relied on to appear when she wasn't wanted. The little girl watched silently as her sister hauled various sweatshirts and jeans out of her wardrobe, finally selecting the newest outfit. Eilidh then brushed her dark hair till it bounced with cleanliness on her shoulders. Having accomplished that, she moved on to the mirror - after all, if this was to be the last time she'd be with Ronnie she might as well look semi-decent. Meanwhile, she tried to ignore Ellis, whose bright eyes were sweeping across the room like some video camera.

Minutes later, both sisters were striding through the garden, past the gold and white and purple flowers that shimmered in the breeze. It was all a riot of colour and Eilidh was pleased to see that Ronnie and her grandfather were examining some of the more unusual flowers. Had they talked of anything else, she wondered. Had her grandfather made his wishes clear? And if so, did Ronnie understand?

Suddenly overtaking her, Ellis became a blur of little limbs, yellow dress flapping. Her own news was so exciting that she wanted the stage to herself without Eilidh to steal her thunder.

"John, Seanair...you know what...Eilidh put lipstick on her eyes! And she left a mess in her room!" She said mess really loud so that her grandfather would be sure to understand the gravity of the offence.

"Shh!" Eilidh hissed. "Your tongue is growing faster than the rest of you - and it wasn't lipstick either!"

Laughing out loud, their grandfather explained to an amused Ronnie, "Our Ellis was raised to be honest, not tactful!" adding, "No longer than an hour now, and keep in mind what I told you."

So they had talked, Eilidh thought, watching as Ronnie nodded solemnly. Nothing more was said till they mounted the motor bike, which was all shiny with newness and very big.

"So what do you think, Eilidh?" Ronnie asked, swivelling round to check her helmet. "Better than my old banger, huh?"

"Definitely," she agreed, "I wouldn't be seen dead riding in that museum piece. I've got my credibility to think of, you know!" Grinning, Ronnie turned back to the business of getting the bike into motion, while Eilidh closed her eyes momentarily in the sunshine and tasted pure pleasure.

Suddenly they were off, and it was just like flying, as they whizzed past garden and greenhouses and trees, then onto the road and into the wide open spaces. Eilidh, with stray bits of hair blowing all over her face, made noises somewhere between laughing and crying. Although Ronnie rode like a maniac - or maybe that was the way all bikers rode - she had a feeling of unwavering happiness. She wanted the experience to last forever. If I could stop time, she thought wildly as the fields flew past them, I would stop it right here, at this moment. Layers of trying to be adult and older-sisterly peeled away and left her, and she whooped with unrestrained delight.

After they had almost gone a full circle, Ronnie slowed down and brought the bike to a halt beside a big steel gate. Jumping off the bike and removing the helmet, he moaned, "would you believe it! These stupid sheep are all over the place - some idiot left the gate open."

Helping a bemused Eilidh off the bike, he asked cheerfully, "Are you any good at chasing sheep? Since Lassie's not here...."

"Wow, can one person cope with such excitement," she retorted with a worldly air. "That must be a real honour, being a stand-in for a sheep dog."

"There! I knew you wouldn't let me down," he said, setting the helmets down beside the bike. "I'll do all the running and you just stand there - yes, there - and make sure they go back in the gate. Dance about, yell, do whatever it takes.

Uncertainly, Eilidh took up her position, calling after him, "I need to have my head examined, agreeing to this."

"S'okay, I know a good therapist," he replied. With that, he sprinted off in the direction of the sheep. Eilidh watched him uneasily, wishing she had checked with him whether sheep bit people or not. John Paterson would not tolerate a sheep within a hundred mile radius of his precious plants, so this would be her very first encounter with the woolly creatures.

After almost ten minutes furiously running to and fro, Ronnie had gathered the twenty-odd sheep together. The flock were now being driven forward, heading in Eilidh's direction. Panicking, she tried to remember the instructions. 'Yell,' he had said. But yell what? What do you say to a stampede of sheep? "In there! Good boy - sorry, girl

- in that gate!" she pleaded coaxingly, but they paid no attention, advancing on her like a storm.

"Clap your hands, Eilidh!" Ronnie shouted at her. "Scream, act hyperactive, do something!" But by now the timing was all wrong, for Eilidh's undignified jumping and yelling only caused the sheep at the front to come to a sudden halt. Alarmed, they then shot sideways, some escaping in the general mayhem, some diving around Eilidh.

"Oh no! Oh Ronnie!" she wailed. "Wait, got this one ...." Lunging to one side, she managed to grab one sheep and hold it by the wool, but it bucked like a donkey, bleated, then pulled itself almost out of her grasp. As Eilidh spun round, gamely trying to hang on, she was only dimly aware of Ronnie hooting and laughing somewhere in the background.

In the next few seconds she was pulled along the springy grass, her brand-new trainers suffering significant damage, her jeans and pink sweatshirt faring little better. She finally landed flat on her back, while the sheep bolted away in disgust, joining up with the splintered flock.

Ronnie, laughing uncontrollably, attempted to pull her to her feet.

"Get off!"

"I'm only helping you!"

"Don't bother only helping...and stop that laughing, will you?" Staggering gracelessly to her feet, she brushed herself down, then looked at Ronnie. His hand was over his mouth, but the heaving shoulders and dancing eyes betrayed him.

"Okay," she said. She held up her dirty hands in a

gesture of mock surrender. "Okay, be my guest, laugh away. Don't mind if I can't join you, but right now, I'm sore in places I didn't know existed." But after a moment, and in spite of her best efforts, she began to laugh and they both doubled up and laughed raucously.

"Macpherson, you really know how to give a girl a good time, don't you?" Eilidh spluttered at last, wiping her eyes.

"I can just see the headlines," said Ronnie, opening an imaginary newspaper, "'Local Hero Lies Legless In A Ditch.'"

The ensuing laughter was cut across by an approaching voice, calling out, "Hallo there!" It was Anna, followed by Paul. "Can we join you?" she sang out.

"It's a free country, isn't it?" Ronnie answered. He said it in such a way that his mood couldn't be guaged, but he had stopped laughing.

Anna, looking long and sleek like a beautiful tigress, came nearer. She had the perfectly-cared-for appearance that suggested hours spent in front of the mirror, the self-approval of the new person she was becoming. Now she appraised Eilidh, studying the battered hairstyle and the dishevelled clothes, then looking briefly at the overall picture again.

"What on earth happened to you, Eilidh?" she cried.

"Phew, you stink, sis!" Paul said cheerfully, putting the knife in further.

Eilidh let that one go by, while Ronnie gave a quick outline of the recent catastrophe. Anna listened to him with a dazzling smile.

'Perhaps I'm misreading the vibes here,' Eilidh thought,

feeling a small frisson of annoyance, 'but is this girl flirting with Ronnie?' Her smile pasted carefully, her mind placed elsewhere, Eilidh listened to Anna's suggestion, "Ronnie, what if you and I go up there, gather the sheep, and Eilidh and Paul can stand on either side of the gate? That should do the trick, shouldn't it?" The sparkling smile was still there, the voice exuding the confidence of a girl who knew just where she stood in the scheme of things.

Listening, Eilidh debated silently, 'It's not that I don't trust you, Anna, it's just that - I don't trust you.'

"No, thanks," Ronnie answered firmly, with a smile in Eilidh's direction, "or this girl will be complaining about slave labour."

"Or Lassie might put forward a complaint to the sheepdog's union," Paul quipped.

Anna's smile dimmed to a reasonable wattage. She groaned, "Stop him someone, before he makes any more corny jokes." Her centrality was becoming so great that she could only function from a position of centre stage. "Oh Ronnie, is that your bike?" she began again in a high-pitched, exclamatory voice. She played up the attentive girl for all it was worth. "Fan-tastic! I've always wanted to ride on one. Pity about this short skirt." Lifting her eyes provocatively from her endless brown legs, she gazed at Ronnie, saying after a moment's pause, "Anyway, who cares? Let's go! It would be the highlight of my holidays, really!"

"I'm a bit whacked," Ronnie said. "Keeping up with Eilidh and sheep is not the recipe for a restful day." He shuffled his feet and stuck his hands in the pocket of his jeans. "Plus, I promised John Paterson I'd have Eilidh home within the hour, right?" Winking at Eilidh, he was rewarded with the ghost of a smile.

Behind the smile, Eilidh suddenly longed to tear her own private fantasy to bits. How could she compete with someone like Anna? Anna, who had changed so much that she could now afford to bask in the high-summer of her teenage beauty. Any female with half an eye could see that she was rapidly turning into a man-eating monster. Problem was, Eilidh supposed, neither Paul nor Ronnie were aware of that.

"C'mon, Ronnie," Anna's brisk voice was saying, "let's go!" Why waste time, her voice seemed to say, on those two irrelevant kids from the city.

Ronnie sighed, said, "Okay, just a five-minute run," then turning to Eilidh he said in a low voice, "Wait for me. We need to talk, you know, about your grandfather...and other things. So, don't go, all right?" Before mounting the bike, he gave her a look which contained its own coded message, but Eilidh just saw what she wanted to see. Anna and Ronnie, together.

As Eilidh watched the bike roar off over the rolling fields, Paul stared at his sister. "Is something on your mind, sis" he said with a broad smile, "or is that a contradiction in terms?"

"Very funny." She played with a long blade of grass where she stood, then yanked it out off the ground saying, "I'm going."

"But he told you to wait!" Paul exclaimed. "Look, Eilidh, I'm not crazy about the guy myself but, for some unknown reason, he really likes you." Almost catching up with her, he gave out a few autocratic messages that she had to wait, couldn't just take off like that....

"Just watch me," she retorted, not looking at him. She wrapped her arms around herself, though the feeling of cold must have come from inside rather than from outside.

"That's a cop-out!" Paul was teasing her, but there was an edge to his voice.

"It's a good cop-out," she answered. A pair of angry grey eyes swivelled brotherward. "I can't stand being around Anna, when she's doing everything apart from licking her lips and drooling over Ronnie."

"Oh my, sensitive aren't we?" He had picked up the vibration instantly, adding, "I don't believe it. You're jealous!"

"Listen to the one who's talking!" Before her mind's eye, she passed a rapid review of Anna's recent treatment of Paul. "I'm not going to wait around and be humiliated, like you. Can't you see? Don't you care? You're nothing more to that...that girl than a railing to grab when her feet give way underneath her. She's using you!" Her pretty face hardened a little, and Paul sensed she was travelling away from him. "I mean, if you're really desperate to turn into a wimp, don't do it in front of me, 'cos I don't know whether to give you a wedge of sympathy or a well-aimed kick. Whatever - I'm not about to make the same mistake!"

The next moment, just as the roar of the motorbike grew louder, she was gone. She had sprinted off towards 'Fasgadh' like a girl with a bus to catch. Paul watched her till she disappeared out of sight. Families would be perfect if it weren't for sisters, he reflected sourly.

Especially one who was warning him that, where Anna was concerned, Paul Alexander was merely marginal to her life.

CHAPTER 14

The green, growing month of June ended, and with it the spell of dry weather. The first day of July, the day after the motorbike fiasco, found Eilidh bleakly staring out of the sitting-room window, where everything beyond it was lost in the blurry miasma of sheeting rain.

"Honestly! February and March and other months are cold and wet, but that's their right. July is plain malicious. You kind of...expect more, don't you?"

"Are you talking about sky's most important product? My plants happen to enjoy it!" her grandfather snorted in disagreement. The shadows on his face wavered a bit with the flickering light of the fire and the darkening that had begun to creep into the room. They both then turned their attention to Ellis who was literally going round in circles.

"Funny how she never seems to have any destination in mind," John observed, trying to catch Ellis, making her giggle. "You just like to be on the move, don't you, honey?"

"Only when it suits herself" Eilidh said, her voice crisp and edged with annoyance. "She was too lazy to put her dirty socks and undies into the washing machine last night so guess where she dumped them? In my school bag, that's where! If I had a hold of you at French today, lady, you'd have been 'finit!' And here I am," she said, turning away from her sister and gesturing to the half-written letter on the desk, "gushing to Cousin Lucille how sweet and lovely Ellis is."

"And not even a mention of all mouth and mayhem! By the way, isn't it time you finished that epistle?" His dark eyes crinkled at the corners as he ruffled Ellis's hair affectionately. "Why don't you tell her about Paul? One minute the romance is over, finished, kaput; and he wants to enter a monastery or go for a degree in solitude. The next moment - like this afternoon - one phone call from Anna and he goes running!"

Eilidh tried hard to imagine Cousin Lucille being even remotely interested in Paul's life. It wasn't easy. "Huh!" she shrugged, "I've given up being a champion of the weak and needy - meaning Paul, of course. He's gone off to town with Anna again," she said, adding silently, 'obviously her self-esteem is so elastic that when Ronnie shows little interest, whoosh, try good old Paul!' Returning to the desk and the letter, she flicked a laughing glance at her grandfather, saying aloud, "Well, I warned him not to try bending MY ear if Anna's rent-a-fan-club resurface. Paul likes to manufacture difficulties, I'm beginning to think. He likes things more complicated than they are!"

Half an hour passed before she slid the letter into the envelope and scooted back the chair away from the mahogany desk. Crossing over to the window, she fixed her eyes hypnotically on the sheets of rain coating the glass and dimming everything outside. She sighed, "I'm just stifled here today."

"Then open a window, my dear."

"Very funny, Seanair. You know exactly what I mean - this is boring!"

"I would say, 'this is nice and peaceful.' A day for some active napping." He slumped down into the arm-chair to prove his point and gazed drowsily at Ellis, who was squatting on the fireside rug.

"And that's where our age gap shows, Seanair." A germ of an idea was beginning to form in Eilidh's mind. "No, I want to get out, see something other than these four walls, etcetera."

John shook his head, as if he'd known all along where Eilidh's words were leading him. "Ah-ha! What's included in the etcetera? Would it be Ronnie, by any chance?"

"Yes, well, sort of." She studied her hands for a moment, a nervous little smile playing over her mouth. "I left him yesterday before we had the chance to talk."

"But he phoned right after," her grandfather said, sitting up like a jack-in-the-box, "and you didn't want to know. Remember?"

"Um, I know, but I thought you'd be annoyed about it." It wasn't exactly the whole truth, and Eilidh heard the words slide from her in the same way that the raindrops were sliding down the glass. She crossed the room and dropped down to where her grandfather was sitting so that they were eye-to-eye. "Seanair, how do you feel about it now?"

"After talking to Ronnie yesterday - fine. He seemed to understand how I felt, you see, and then I realised I was punishing him because he was Roderick Macpherson's son." Putting his hand lightly on her arm, he added, "So, all those warnings to you, well, just put them down to another silly day in my life. As they say in the States, my judgment wasn't too sharp there!"

Oblivious to the serious discussion, Ellis lifted a flushed face from the warmth of the fire and turned her attention to the television. She fiddled with the controls while her grandfather continued speaking. "I panicked at the thought of you finding out about the accident from Ronnie's father, Eilidh, and that you'd say nothing to me about it but...but you'd start seeing me in a different way." There was still the small echo of sadness in his voice as he played up the word 'different'.

"Well, I see you differently all right, but not in the way you mean." She shifted her weight back and forth gently on the carpeted floor. "You're different because I can see you with new eyes - ."

"Oh, no, you're preaching again!" John had a hard time looking tough so he gave her an affectionate hug instead. "Go on, get in touch with Ronnie - you know what phones are for, don't you?"

She felt herself blushing, especially when she realised that she had been gripping hard the side of his armchair. She let go and felt where the hard wooden edge of the chair had dug into her palms. She had wanted his approval that much. And now, the fact that he understood her, believed in her, because he knew her, made Eilidh's heart swell up with warmth. And the looking-forwardness of that phone call made her feel as if the sun was rising up inside her.

Too much so. So much, that it frightened her, and she hesitated. Instead of getting up, she stared absently at the increasing rain outside. The windows were now awash like scenes from a Hollywood thriller where technicians played hoses on to the action.

"Ellis, get your dirty little hands off the T.V. screen," she ordered, trying a spot of diversional therapy.

"But my dirty little hands are clean," Ellis called back with a captivating smile. John laughed at this, and then stared at Eilidh in silence for some seconds before saying, "honest answer, Eilidh - why the hesitation?"

Eilidh would not meet his eyes. "Hesitation?" she repeated.

"You know what I mean." He turned in the chair and confronted her. "A few minutes ago you were desperate to get in touch with Ronnie again - now the brakes are on. Why?"

She shook her head a little before answering. "I don't know. I mean, I don't know how to explain."

"Eilidh, I didn't shut you out last week when I was telling you about the accident, did I? And I didn't have the right words either."

Eilidh and her grandfather stared at each other fully for a minute while Ellis unsuccessfully attempted a somersault.

"It's just that," Eilidh began, "the way I was looking forward to hearing Ronnie's voice - y'know, when he'd answer the phone - well, it frightened me."

"Frightened you?"

"Yeah, like there was suddenly a warning bell or a neon sign saying 'don't care so much. Don't care about anyone so much.'"

"Why?" The word was small, and he turned to Eilidh, repeating quietly, "why?"

"Don't really know. I think...." Embarrassed, she lowered her lids and shifted her body minutely. She forced herself to look up again, saying, "I think, when Mum died, something slammed shut inside me - does that sound stupid? See, I loved Mum so much, and it hurt too much and I don't want that hurt again."

"So you decided, unconsciously, never to love anyone as much as you loved your mum." He paused; then, his voice low, he asked, "too risky? Is that it?"

"Suppose so." 'And,' she had to admit silently to herself, 'I don't want to be hurt the way Anna is hurting Paul.'

"Yes, Eilidh," her grandfather said, after a while, "love makes you vulnerable, right enough. There's all this need thing for a start. Needing to see that person, needing to hear their voice...and all that. It opens you up to hurt, doesn't it?"

"Uh-huh. What bugs me is"- the worry was deep in her voice as she tried to explain - "what if I let myself care for Ronnie...and he's taken away, too? Or he lets me down?"

"Then your faith must be the well-diluted kind, Eilidh." Turning away from her, he picked up a newspaper, adding, "it isn't strong enough for the real world." There was a bite to the last words.

Her head jerked up at this. Once again, she had come face to face with the idea of a God who could say, it's alright...whatever happens, I'll be there.

She faced her grandfather in mock fierceness. "Hey, who's preaching now?" She laughed, and John Paterson laughed with her.

"Don't worry, I'll quit while behind," he said, his voice always sounding more American when he used their slang. "Now, can I read this paper in peace....?"

The phone call only took a minute. When she came back into the room, her grey eyes were worried, her face set with thought. "Did you get through?" her grandfather enquired, pausing in some serious Lego construction work. Ellis, kneeling in front of him, was lost with silent absorption in the miracle of manufacture which was taking place right before her eyes.

"Eilidh, did you get through?" John Paterson repeated.

"Yeah, but, " she leaned her back against the living room door, "Mrs Macpherson sounded awfully worried - seems that Ronnie went off to look for a missing sheep. He thought it might have got tangled up in that fence near Creag Dubh. That was three hours ago."

John whistled his surprise. "Shouldn't take him that long. Has his father gone looking for him?"

"No, he's broken his ankle. And Mrs Macpherson ...well, she thought he was here. Ronnie said that he was going to see me. And, of course, when she realized I was looking for him, well, she went into a blind panic. She said she was off to search for him, and just slammed down the phone." Eilidh's voice was getting faster and faster as she replayed Mrs Macpherson's high-pitched words 'Then WHERE is he?!'

Wasting no further time, she left the room and bounded up the stairs to her bedroom. Two minutes later, and still struggling into her green wax cotton jacket, she made her way back down the stairs. Her grandfather's presence at the bottom of the steps made her stop in her tracks.

She saved him the trouble of questioning. "I'm going out. You don't mind keeping an eye on Ellis, do you? I - ."

"Actually, I do mind. You see, I'm going out to look for Ronnie."

"But that's where I was going!" Eilidh's mouth drooped down a little at the ends as she held onto the bannister.

"Hold the 'buts' and don't arrange that bonnie face into a pout. Oh, I know exactly what you're thinking - that you'd like to be the one to find him, yes? You've got such an expressive face, Eilidh. Your thoughts are written all over your face!" Leaning forward with a degree of urgency, he said, "But I know the coastal area like the back of my hand. You don't. All right, so he may only be sheltering somewhere out of this storm, but, at least, I know the places he might pick. So you stay here. All right?" The command behind the words were unmistakable.

Eilidh tried to neutralise the sullenness that she felt was masking her face. "All right...but I feel I want to DO something!"

"You can pray, can't you?" he said, sewing up the argument. And, for just a moment, Eilidh could see into her grandfather's eyes. There had been a look of longing in them, which he erased the minute she nodded in agreement.

"Don't waste any time!" she called after his retreating back, and he answered with, "I'm already out!"

She moved back into the living room, now soft with the gentle tones of firelight. While she built a Lego tower with Ellis, the rain continued its slow patternless tattoo on the roof and, in the distance, the solemn drum-roll of thunder sounded. It was Eilidh's first experience of a summer thunder-storm on the island, and she felt oddly alone, depite Ellis's noisy presence.

As the afternoon dragged, the clock seemed to slow down. Even its quarter-hour chimes were mournful. For Eilidh, the waiting seemed to press on her temples and shoulders like some burden weighted down with rocks of fear. She didn't know how much longer she could just sit there, playing games with Ellis, and being uneasy.

She sent her thoughts upwards. 'I don't have to carry all this uneasiness by myself, do I?' Reaching for the family Bible she read Ellis one of her own favourite verses, 'cast all your anxiety on him because he cares for you.' What a fantastic, incomprehensible, feeling! God of Gods; King of Kings; Jesus, Name of all Majesty; Jesus, the outshining of God: He was all that, yet, he cared for HER! She rushed out her thoughts in a prayer because she was glad to have peace. Peace in the face of the whole constellation of fears that threatened to possess her. Peace. Tons of it. She could, she thought with some amusement, can a supply of it for hard times, but...she didn't have to. It would always be there.

"Thank you," she whispered. "Thank you that you're in charge of Ronnie at this moment. Thank you." Eilidh found that deep gratitude, like deep joy, was almost impossible to express. Suddenly, she knew what her next move should be.

CHAPTER 15

Having made up her mind what to do next, Eilidh turned to her sister. Ellis was busily using her sleeve to mop up spilt Ribena. Accompanying the furious movements was some muttered self-reproach. "How COULD you! How-could-you!"

"Oh Ellis, you frighten me," Eilidh laughed, giving her sister a squeeze. "You're more like me than I am! C'mon, get your rain coat and wellies. I think the rain is easing off, so we can go down to the Macpherson's. Better than hanging out here, isn't it?"

Ellis gave her answer in an ecstatic whirl and in a few minutes she was buttoned up in her yellow raincoat. "There, lovey," Eilidh said, pulling the hood over the shiny curls, "you're all wrapped up now."

"Like a present?"

Laughing, Eilidh agreed, "that's right, like a present! C'mon, let's go."

Outside in the pale, ethereal, water-colour world, the raindrops were still describing complex circular designs in the puddles. The rain was no longer torrential and the storm had lost its intensity, but the trees were, as Ellis said, still fighting together. The sea continued cavorting in an astonishing way. It was now frothing crazily in the

137

wind, its immensity compelling.

The two sisters marched determinedly over the soggy
ground, rather like two spies on a desperate mission. At
the Macpherson's house there was no answer to Eilidh's
knock, and after a while, she opened the frosted glass
door. They both slipped into the utility room with its
colourful rugs and teracotta floor tiles.

"Ronnie, Ronnie! - is that you?" a voice called from
somewhere in the house and they followed the sound.
Eilidh peeped into the living room, which was an
imaginative mesh of old and new; good modern furniture
sitting happily with antique and hand-me-down pieces. In
a corner of the room sat Roderick Macpherson by the
phone, two crutches propped beside his chair and his
ankle encased in plaster. His face, although handsome
and filled with character, was not warm or welcoming.
Rather, it registered disappointment.

"Oh! Oh...I thought it might be Ronnie." His voice
sounded hoarse, strangely disused. "You haven't seen
him, have you?"

"No, Mr Macpherson. That's why I came. To see if he
had turned up."

He shook his head, motioned for them to sit down, and
lit a cigarette. Taking a deep puff he said, "By the way,
just call me Roddy."

'Never,' thought Eilidh and sat down on the black
leather sofa. Mr Macpherson attempted some baby talk
with Ellis who merely gazed at the ceiling in lofty
withdrawal. Eventually the little girl decided to converse
with the black cat who snoozed beside the unwatched and
mute face of the T.V. set; but Eilidh could tell from the

heaviness in her lap that her sister would soon join the cat in the world of dreams.

The blue smoke hung in the air between them until Mr Macpherson finally turned to Eilidh. "I've phoned round everyone I can think of, and they haven't seen Ronnie. A couple of the men said they would go out looking for him if he hadn't returned by night-time. Fat lot of good that'll do!" As he stubbed out the half-smoked cigarette, Eilidh glanced at the man sitting hunched, staring at the blazing fire but not really seeing it. The hours of waiting had left a bleak and helpless man, or had his inner landscape always been like that? Eilidh wondered. She wriggled Ellis into a more comfortable position in her lap.

In the face of the man's despair, Eilidh's reasoned, don't-rock-the-boat approach evaporated. "My grand-father - John - " she said, "went looking for Ronnie after I phoned here."

Instead of the look of sour disbelief and unmistakable distrust she had anticipated, Eilidh saw the man's eyes close momentarily. But not before she registered the expression of pain in them. All at once, she felt immediately that there was something wrong about him. But...how to define what was the matter? It made her uneasy, because it was a total wrongness. Was he an emotional cripple, just another piece of human flotsam, tossed back and forth on a sea of hate - or was there something deeper at issue here?

They sat on in the oppressive silence, Ellis sleeping soundly, Mr Macpherson continuing to chain smoke, fidget, sigh, or look at the television in an abstracted way. At the sound of the front door bursting open, he made a strange noise, something between an outcry and an exhale. "Oh God, please let it be - ."

"Roddy! Oh Roddy!" Mrs Macpherson flung open the living room door, her clothes drenched, her blonde hair flopping over her face, her eyes wild. "Our poor, poor Ronnie...oh, it's so awful!"

"You found him? W-what - ."

"Where? Where is he?" Eilidh interrupted the Macphersons.

"At Creag Dubh, of all places! I can't believe this is happening," and Mrs Macpherson made sweeping gestures with her forearm, shrieking, "what are we going to do? What are we going to do?"

The hysterical last words seemed to signal action, like the gunshot at the start of a race. Eilidh dumped her sleeping sister unceremoniously on the couch, while Mr Macpherson struggled onto his crutches, gulping air as if he had used up a lot of energy. "Is he...is he all right?" he asked, in a hoarse-sounding whisper.

"I don't know! I just don't know! He's lying awfully still."

"What happened? Won't you tell us! What happened to him?" Eilidh all but screamed, feeling as if her head would explode.

"He must have fallen or slipped over the edge of Creag Dubh. Maybe it's eroded there, or maybe it was slippery...I don't know. He landed on some ledge -" Mrs Macpherson was shaking violently, and it was becoming more difficult to understand her quavering voice. "We were shouting down at him but, even if he is conscious, he wouldn't hear us with the noise of the sea. John Paterson says we've got to get help to him right away because - Oh Roddy - the water's rising!"

CHAPTER 16

Eilidh took a deep breath. She heard Mrs Macpherson's words, heard them deep inside her. And even as she heard Ronnie's mother frantically dialling 999 for the coastguards; even as she heard the almost incoherent instuctions being shouted down the phone to several neighbours - loudly, as though the wires were powerless on their own; even then, Eilidh felt as if she was being held on the edge of a dream.

The dreamlike feeling was reinforced by Roderick Macpherson's subsequent actions.

At first, he had sat down heavily, his eyes seeming unconnected, unreachable, but then he began to shake his head violently from side to side, as though denying his wife's words. "No," he said, "Not Ronnie. Not my boy." He reached for the crutches again, gripping them to steady himself as he got up. The knuckles of his weather-beaten hands turned white. "Not my boy," he repeated.

And then he whispered something Eilidh didn't catch.

Mrs Macpherson's voice drifted in from the hall, rising in fresh hysteria as two neighbours walked in. "...and John Paterson is his only chance! He's tied a rope to the fence post and he's lowering himself down...he thought he could maybe drag Ronnie further up the ledge...give him more time before the tide -   Oh, let's go, let's go!"

She hurried into the room, followed by two neigh-bours, one of which was Anna's father. George Murray brought with him a master of the universe self-regard which suggested he found even this crisis easy. "Don't worry, Roddy," he said soothingly, "we'll soon have the boy home."

"How can you say that?" Mrs Macpherson shouted. "You haven't even seen where he's lying, have you? You don't know how impossible - "

Mrs Macpherson stopped in mid sentence as she heard her husband's words. "It's my fault! It's all my fault!" He pounded on the nearby wall with one hand, crashing down each syllable.

"How can it be your fault, Roddy? Don't be so daft!" His wife's voice overrode Mr Macpherson, by dint of exasperation rather than volume.

"Because it's a judgment on me, Jean, that's why!" he said passionately, his voice lashing her. Slamming his fist into the wall again, he said, "Because it was MY fault little Peter got killed, and I let Paterson take the blame, all these years. That's why! And now my son is paying the price. Because of me!"

The two men made combined noises of shock while Eilidh tried to throw off the confusion that now clogged her tongue. She knew that no question she had ever asked before, or would ever ask again, would match the effort of getting this one sentence out. "Mr Macpherson, what...what exactly do you mean?"

"I hated Paterson. He had everything, that fancy

Morris Minor, and then...the only girl I c-cared for...."
He stumbled on the last few words, looked at his wife, and
then took several deep breaths before continuing. "I'm
sorry, Jean, but that was long, long ago. Long before I met
you. But I wanted to teach Paterson a lesson. So I fiddled
with the brakes - opened up the brake-pipe nozzle...just
wanted that precious car of his damaged, you know?"
The plea in his voice begged them all to understand.
"How was I to know that Peter would...would...."

His voice tailed off and he and his wife stood face to
face. Jean Macpherson then looked downwards, apparently studying her husband's plaster-cast. Slowly, her
gaze travelled up to her husband's face and Eilidh felt her
asking the same unspoken questions that were on her own
mind.

Instead, Mrs Macpherson shook her head as if to
dislodge his revelation from her mind. Her locked features
stayed locked, and when she spoke, her voice was cold.
"We'll talk about this later, Roddy. Right now, it's a total
waste of time."

Roderick Macpherson flinched as if his wife had
slapped him. She turned and went out of the room, leaving
him. He stood staring at the place where she had been.

The two men, who had reeled with shock at the
confession, now busied themselves with pulling on oilskin
jackets. Then they were gone, leaving Eilidh with Roderick
Macpherson.

She didn't know what to say. She didn't even, she
recognised with impotent fury, know what she wanted to
say.

"Eilidh, please. Please try and forgive me - ." White-faced, and with the lines round his mouth sagging with defeat, Mr Macpherson began to speak.

"No!"

"Please, try - ."

"Mr Macpherson, what part of the word 'no' don't you understand? Huh?" Eilidh zeroed in on the man's weakest moment, her voice filled with disgust. "So, yesterday's caught up with you at last, has it? Are you so blind? Can't you see? Your sorrow may be real enough, but it's years too late, miles too short. And - and if you think I won't tell my grandfather about this, you can dream on!"

"How can I make you understand when I hardly understand it myself?" the man cried out in protest. "That night wee Peter was killed, part of me died with him. And that's not being over-sentimental. That's the way it was...is! And when everyone assumed Paterson was to blame, I jumped on the bandwagon...it was the only way I could keep my sanity. All these years, it's been the only way I could cope. To deny it, to repress it, to blame someone else for...." He choked on his words and his eyes welled up, and he broke down completely.

By now, Eilidh had had enough of this conversation. She was tired of hearing this man administering himself with...with some psychological pain-killers, some moral purgative. He could wrap up his can-of-worms in all the psychiatric jargon of denial, repression, or whatever label came to hand. He could wrap it up in any pretty colour he liked, for all she cared. Right now, she was too busy building up a head of steam, and she wanted to run it off.

"Mr Macpherson, please spare us the psycha- " she

stumbled, having trouble with the pronounciation, "psy-chological explanations. If my grandfather slips down that rock, then...you'll get the pay-off you've been wait-ing for all these years, won't you? Anyway, your wife is right. All this is a total waste of time. You can look after Ellis, can't you? Because I'm off!"

She ran out of the house and didn't stop running till she neared the steep incline leading to Creag Dubh. Out of breath, her chest heaving, she stood there. In the greyness of the land, in the vastness of it, she stood still. Turning her collar up against the cold, she shoved her hands into the pockets of her jacket and waited for her heart to resume its normal pattern. The sky was gloomy, with masses of rain-heavy clouds bunched in the west; the only sound was the faint whisper and moan of the dying breeze. She filled her lungs with energizing sea air. Another few yards to go and she would see the first signs of the desperate rescue.

'As salt are we ready to savour in darkness are we ready to be light.'

The sudden words of her favourite chorus brought a cold, sick feeling over her which made her shut her eyes against her destination. The recognition of what she had just done washed around inside her mind. How could she go on, when she had said so many damaging, unforgiving things? How could SHE be light in the darkness, when she had shown she was no different from anyone else? When she had completely shut off herself from a man's agony over the past, and now, over the present?

Jesus had been HER stand-in, on Calvary. And still she so easily forgot.

To find out the depths of her own hardness was a discovery as crushing as the discovery of Roderick Macpherson's actions. She felt her eyes aching unbearably, and she wanted to cry, for herself.

"Oh God, forgive me. Jesus, make me like you."

CHAPTER 17

For Eilidh, it was the easiest thing in the world to go back to Roderick Macpherson and ask his forgiveness. And he had been so grateful, that Eilidh felt strangely touched. There was something infinitely moving and pathetic about that gratitude. But there was no time to dwell on it and soon she was on the run again, her trainers squishing with each step, her feet flying effortlessly, skimming over the rain-spangled grass. This time she didn't stop till she saw the huddled group of people on the cliff top.

At the horizon, she could see the line between sky and sea as blurred and indefinite. The sea itself was still grey and foaming, and as she joined the others at the edge of the cliff, she was almost hypnotised by the dizzying rush of water pounding below. The heavy spray from the sea, crashing over the rocks, swirled up towards the cliff top like a gossamer mist.

The sudden fine wetness shocked Eilidh and helped her to focus. Keeping well away from the eroded part of the cliff-top, she flattened herself against the damp ground, screwed up her eyes, and looked downwards. She could just make out the crumpled form of Ronnie on a grassy ledge some distance below them. Edging cautiously towards Ronnie, just inches away from a fatal plunge, was her grandfather. He had a thick rope tied round his waist.

"He's going to pull Ronnie further up the ledge, away from the rising water," Anna's father explained.

'And one false step on that slippery surface...and he'll be right over the edge,' thought Eilidh, 'and then these boulders and that boiling foam - Oh, Seanair!'

Her heart cramped up tight and she had not one thought in her head except being afraid. No please please no! her mind said over and over again, like some litany. If only there was just something she could do.

Only of course there was. She saw instantly and sharply what there was for her to do, and once again that day, screwed her eyes tight shut. Jesus was just a prayer away.

"Look! Ronnie's moving his head. Or is he? No, he's so still! Oh, I wish I could see better - " Mrs Macpherson's voice wasn't working right, so low it was almost drowned out by an indistinct buzzing sound somewhere in the distance. As they waited and watched, the buzzing sound grew louder and louder, nearer and nearer, until, overhead, they could hear the chattering noise of a helicopter.

In an instant, the wokka-wokka-wokka noise was everywhere. The rhythm of the helicopter's flashing lights played along with Eilidh's thumping heart, making a complex, scary beat. The twin rotor blades beat the air above them, creating a hurricane-type downwash which lifted Eilidh's hair madly round her head. It flailed the grass on the cliff top, and worse still, blew loose bits of cliff face down in the direction of the ledge.

Beside Eilidh, Mrs Macpherson whispered, "Oh no - oh no - oh no...." Then she stood, her hands to her mouth, smothering a scream.

Eilidh tried to stand, too, but her legs betrayed her. She wanted them to get up, and move, but her knees weren't having any of it. Finally moving into a kneeling position, Eilidh gestured in the direction of the rapidly rising helicopter and shouted to Anna's father, "W-why is the helicopter going up and away like that?"

"I think it's something to do with the updraft," Mr Murray yelled back. "The sea breeze hits the cliff and - whoosh - it's problems for the 'copter! They're getting blown upwards."

At this, Mrs Macpherson clapped her hand on her ears and rocked sideways in anguish. "They're not...not giving up, are they? Surely not!" Raw agony filled her eyes as they followed the helicopter, at first circling overhead, and then moving towards the sea, pointing into the wind. "They're going! They're giving up! They can't do - " The words were lost in a torrent of tears, and she held her face in her hands, and sobbed.

Eilidh felt she ought to say something, but nothing presented itself. In the now-tense near quiet, her brain had decided to shut down. Feeling her fingernails digging savagely into the palms of her hand, she tried to understand Mr Murray's now gentle explanation. "...so you see, Jean, the rescue crew have to hold off somewhere out of the disturbed air. They have to plan, and talk. They have to pull away from causing further damage to Ronnie and John - you know, with falling stones and that - but they will come back, only from a different angle. Do you understand?"

Jean Macpherson nodded mutely, and lifted her head again, this time to see the helicopter moving backwards, moving above and away from the mad turmoil of the waves, manoeuvring gently towards the cliff face. Despite the movement, Eilidh felt that the whole scene in front of her was clamped into hostile solidity. Even the sea and sky, forged together in savagery, lashed by wild winds, even that now seemed frozen in time. Disaster had a strange way of making everything timeless.

And yet a lifetime seemed to pass before the winchman made his descent on the winchwire. As he was lowered to about forty feet over the sea, the helicopter climbed higher and higher. For a moment, Eilidh lost sight of the winchman altogether, but then, there he was, now in contact with the cliff face, feet in front, easing up the cliff face. It looked a bit like abseiling in reverse.

As the helicopter moved away, back towards the sea, a knife-edge quiet settled over the onlookers. And Eilidh thought of the three men on that ledge, and of how two of them had got so woven into her life, that if they weren't in it - but she couldn't, wouldn't, picture the design of her life without them.

Everyone's eyes were now fixed on the drama taking place below, waiting. A whole five minutes elapsed, slowly. Another five minutes. Nothing. And then Eilidh could bear it no longer. "What's happening now?" she asked.

"Well, the 'copter fellow," - Mr Murray was group commentator - "I think he's still attached to a slack cable, well, he'll look Ronnie over, and radio the crew.... Ah yes, that was smart! Look, they're lowering the stretcher and a box - First Aid, I suppose...." The running commentary died away. Time passed, minutes lasting forever.

And then Eilidh thought she saw Ronnie being strapped onto a whitish stretcher, shaped almost like a coffin-lid, and being lifted by a suspension harness. Stretcher and winchman were winched away from the cliff face, down towards the sea and those white-capped waves. Then, in unison, the onlookers lifted their eyes higher, higher still, drawn as if by some magnetic force towards the tiny figures silhouetted against the sky, as both rescued and rescuer were pulled up towards the helicopter. And in just another eye-blink both men were being pulled through its open door.

"Thank you, Lord," Eilidh whispered, watching the lights flashing in the air as the helicopter whirled its way through the greyish solitude of the sky. The lights then winked distinctly across the sea, while the onlookers on the cliff top bear-hugged each other. After that, it was all rapid, decisive, powerful movements as they began to pull the rope-harnessed John Paterson back up the cliff face.

CHAPTER 18

For ever afterwards, Eilidh would remember how the men pulled and pulled at that rope, their knuckles showing white, their grunting and heaving seeming louder as the helicopter's chatter faded away into the distance. And how a watery sun briefly bathed the land in its light just as John Paterson was hauled to safety.

Both Mrs Macpherson and Eilidh leapt up to help him into a lying-down position.

"Seanair! Are you okay?"

"John - how's Ronnie?" Although Mrs Macpherson's voice was controlled, there was a husky, animal-like quality in her voice. "How bad is he? How - ."

An autocratic voice stopped the questions dead. "Give him a chance, will you?" Mr Murray said. "Can't you see he's done in?"

They could, and both females traded hangdog looks. John Paterson, now lying on the damp grass, had been reduced, mentally and physically, almost to his last component of endurance. It looked like every cell enclosed in his tall frame wanted to curl up and go to sleep. Ripples ran along his body, and choking, coughing sounds came from him as he tried to get rid of inhaled grit. Eilidh, leaning over and plucking agitatedly at his sleeve, studied his face, the glistening dark-red globule marking out a forehead injury; the dark shadows like bruises under his eyes; the lines of weariness enclosing the mouth.

She was startled when his eyes flickered open and he nodded a 'yes' to both herself and Mrs Macpherson. For a long moment he stared straight at them, as if in two minds whether to say more or retreat back into his exhaustion.

"Oh, Seanair, I was praying so hard for you and Ronnie," Eilidh said softly, in a voice that was a hair away from a cry.

"You and me both, then," John Paterson squeezed the words out.

"Did Ronnie manage to speak? Was he conscious?" Mrs Macpherson cried. "He looked so still!"

"That's because he was stunned - " He shivered involuntarily and his voice trailed off into silence. But Mrs Macpherson kept probing him, kept pushing him relentlessly. Her face quivered with the need to know, and then John Paterson's eyes met hers; and his compassion was total, instantaneous.

"It could have been a lot worse...the clumpy grass on that ledge saved Ronnie. His shoulder or arm may be broken, and maybe some ribs. I don't know, I'm no doctor." He swallowed and carried on with some effort. "At any rate, he can move both legs, and one arm."

"Oh, thank you, thank you!" Mrs Macpherson repeated over and over again in a breathless rush.

"But why didn't you go on the helicopter, Seanair?" Eilidh's voice broke in.

"I'm a hundred per-cent stubborn, isn't that what you

said yourself?" His smile had a tremulous edge as he added, "And I hate hospitals!"

Neither Mrs Macpherson nor Eilidh smiled in return. They were both thinking of what must be spoken. A muscle was jumping near Mrs Macpherson's mouth as she spoke. "John...John, my husband's got something important to tell you. So, just as soon as the doctor's checked you over, I'll make sure Roddy'll be brought over to see you."

Keep your heart open for your husband, Eilidh pleaded silently, looking at the older woman. The shivering form lying beside her suddenly refocused her attention. A Range Rover to collect him, and a doctor to care for him, were both on their way, but in the meantime John Paterson badly needed warmth.

Knowing that she was young and strong and could withstand the damp cold better than the other helpers, she pulled off her overjacket and thick sweatshirt and wrapped them round his body. Despite shivering now in her cotton T-shirt, she felt better at having taken a positive-action decision. Changing position slightly, she managed to cradle her grandfather's head in her arms.

The drizzle had tapered off, but the wind still came in gusts, and the clouds raced one another across the rain-washed sky. There was a clean fresh smell in the air of washed stones and grass, and the sharp, trilling sounds of birdlife came down to her clearly as they chattered on the wing.

In her arms, John Paterson was saying. "...and is it as simple as that? A turning point in the right direction, one small moment when you KNOW?"

"What's that, Seanair?"

"When I was down there...." The words were dragged from a bottomless well of exhaustion. "I thought of how my action would breach the divide between me and the Macpherson's. And then, I saw it all as clearly as if it had been printed on a page...I saw how Christ's action, his death on the cross, had breached the divide between God and man. And I believed."

"Oh, Seanair!"

Tears sprang to Eilidh's eyes, and she felt soaked in joy. She allowed her thoughts to wander along with the clouds, following one another, going nowhere, and yet...going somewhere. She remembered her mother. No way would she ever forget her.

Remembering hurt, but it was a good kind of hurt. Her mother hadn't wanted her children to have a future as smooth as silk, with no snags, no hang-ups. That wasn't reality. What she had wanted for them was the removal of that soft bitterness, the planting of a faith that had survival value, the clothing with joy.

Eilidh's thought drifted, briefly, to Paul; chasing Anna, chasing romance, chasing the wind. And then to Ronnie. She thought of those desperate hours when death must have seemed to him so close. And she allowed herself to care.

The sun came out once again and this time flooded the sky with a gentle warmth and glow. The raindrops, still held by the short, springy grass, sprinkled like tiny diamonds.

"Seanair?" she said. "Seanair, see how innocent the land looks! Right now, you'd never believe there was such a thing as a storm."